Praise for **Yellow Back Radio Broke-Down**

"Literary surrealism has invaded Marlboro Country. . . . Reed skins all our sacred cows. He scalps every hero who wanders by. He turns the American West into a ribald hell where iron-jawed hogs eat people, the devil swings like a hopped-up defrocked padre, and the great emissaries of Christian doctrine behave like a purple-robed Mafia. Ishmael Reed has mastered the vocabulary of blasphemy."

—*Life Magazine*

"A wild and wicked burlesque and free-wheeling fantasy. . . . The American scene, past and present, with all its inconsistencies and white vanity, takes it on the chin and so does Christianity, for the Loop Garoo Kid, it turns out, is not only a black superman, but the devil incarnate—and he's a-winnin' out."

—*Publishers Weekly*

"Ishmael Reed is a most talented humorist and possessor of a powerfully antic and lyric imagination. . . . *Yellow Back Radio Broke-Down* should be read as hard evidence of Reed's uncommon talent."

—*New Yorker*

"*Yellow Back Radio Broke-Down* is a full blown 'horse opera,' a surrealistic spoof of the Western with Indian chiefs aboard helicopters, stagecoaches and closed circuit TVs, cavalry charges of taxis."

—*New York Review of Books*

BY ISHMAEL REED

ESSAYS

Writin' Is Fightin'
God Made Alaska for the Indians
Shrovetide in Old New Orleans
Airing Dirty Laundry

NOVELS

Japanese by Spring
The Terrible Threes
Reckless Eyeballing
The Terrible Twos
Flight to Canada
The Last Days of Louisiana Red
Mumbo Jumbo
Yellow Back Radio Broke-Down
The Free-Lance Pallbearers

POETRY

New and Collected Poems
A Secretary to the Spirits
Chattanooga
Conjure
Catechism of D Neoamerican Hoodoo Church

PLAYS

Mother Hubbard, *formerly* Hell Hath No Fury
The Ace Boons
Savage Wilds
Hubba City

ANTHOLOGIES

The Before Columbus Foundation Fiction Anthology
The Before Columbus Foundation Poetry Anthology
Calafia
19 Necromancers from Now
Multi-America: Essays on Cultural War and Cultural Peace

Yellow Back Radio
Broke-Down

ISHMAEL REED

Dalkey Archive Press

Library of Congress Cataloging-in-Publication Data:

Reed, Ishmael, 1938-
      Yellow back radio broke-down / Ishmael Reed. — 1st Dalkey Archive ed.
          p.   cm.
      ISBN 1-56478-238-7 (alk. paper)
       1. Afro-American cowboys—Fiction. 2. West (U.S.)—Fiction. I. Title.
PS3568.E365 Y4 2000
813'.54—dc21   00-020976

This publication is partially supported by grants from the Lannan Foundation and the Illinois Arts Council, a state agency.

Dalkey Archive Press
www.dalkeyarchive.com

To Carla, Pope Joan and Dancer
my 3 Wangols

CONTENTS

YELLOW BACK RADIO BROKE-DOWN

I. The Loop Garoo Kid Goes Away Mad

I was content. I was surrounded by no greedy grafters, no slimy creatures. Just dogs, horses, sheep, goats, bulls, burros and Men.

William S. Hart

America . . . is just like a turkey. It's got white meat and it's got dark meat. They is different, but they is both important to the turkey. I figure the turkey has more white meat than dark meat, but that don't make any difference. Both have nerves running through 'em. I guess Hoo-Doo is a sort of nerve that runs mostly in the dark meat, but sometimes gets into the white meat, too.

. . . Anywhere they go my people know the signs.

Henry Allen

Oh, the hoodoos have chased me and still I am not broke,
I'm going to the mountains and think I am doing well;
I am going to the mountains some cattle for to sell,
And I hope to see the hoodoos dead and damn them all in hell.

from "The Rustler," an American cowboy song

Folks. This here is the story of the Loop Garoo Kid. A cowboy so bad he made a working posse of spells phone in sick. A bullwhacker so unfeeling he left the print of winged mice on hides of crawling women. A desperado so onery he made the Pope cry and the most powerful of cattlemen shed his head to the Executioner's swine.

A terrible cuss of a thousand shivs he was who wasted whole herds, made the fruit black and wormy, dried up the water holes and caused people's eyes to grow from tiny black dots into slapjacks wherever his feet fell.

Now, he wasn't always bad, trump over hearts diamonds and clubs. Once a wild joker he cut the fool before bemused Egyptians, dressed like Mortimer Snerd and spilled french fries on his lap at Las Vegas' top of the strip.

Booted out of his father's house after a quarrel, whores snapped at his heels and trick dogs did the fandango on his belly. Men called him brother only to cop his coin and tell malicious stories about his cleft foot.

Born with a caul over his face and ghost lobes on his ears, he was a mean night tripper who moved from town to town quoting Thomas Jefferson and allowing bandits to build a flophouse around his genius.

A funny blue hippo who painted himself with water
flowers only to be drummed out of each tribe dressed
down publicly, his medals ripped off.

● ○

Finally he joined a small circus and happily performed
with his fellow 86-D—a Juggler a dancing Bear a fast
talking Barker and Zozo Labrique, charter member of
the American Hoo-Doo Church.

Their fame spread throughout the frontier and bouquets
of flowers greeted them in every town until they moved
into that city which seemed a section of Hell chipped off
and shipped upstairs, Yellow Back Radio, where even the
sun was afraid to show its bottom.

● ○

Some of the wheels of the caravan were stuck in thick
red mud formed by a heavy afternoon downpour. The
oxen had to be repeatedly whipped. They had become
irritable from the rain which splashed against their faces.
In the valley below black dust rose in foreboding clouds
from herds of wild horses that roamed there. Loop Garoo
was driving the horse hitched to Zozo Labrique's
covered wagon.

Those were some dangerous stunts you did in the last
town, boy, bucking those killer broncos like that. A few

more turns with that bull and you would have been really
used up. Why you try so hard?

She sent me a letter in the last town, Zozo. She wants me
to come to her. The old man spends his time grooming
his fur and posing for non-academic painters. He's more
wrapped up in himself than ever before and the other
one, he's really gone dipso this time. Invites winos up
there who pass the bottle and make advances on her.
Call her sweet stuff and honey bun—she's really in hard
times. She's a constant guest in my dreams Zozo, her face
appears the way she looked the night she went uptown
on me.

Serves her right Loop, the way she treated you. And that
trash she collected around her. They were all butch. As
soon as she left, zoom they were gone. And that angel
in drag like a john, he gave her the news and showed her
her notices—right off it went to her head. When she humiliated you—that emboldened the others to do likewise.
Mustache Sal deserted you and Mighty Dike teamed up
with that jive fur trapper who's always handing you
subpoenas. You know how they are, Loop, you're the original pimp, the royal stud—soon as a bottom trick finds
your weakness your whole stable will up and split.

I let her open my nose Zozo. I should have known that if
she wasn't loyal to him with as big a reputation as he had
—I couldn't expect her to revere me. What a line that guy
had. A mitt man from his soul. And her kissing his
feet just because those three drunken reporters were
there to record it. Ever read their copy on that event
Zozo? It's as if they were all witnessing something en-
tirely different. The very next night she was in my bunk

gnashing her teeth and uttering obscenities as I climbed
into her skull.

She got to your breathing all right Loop. Even the love
potions you asked me to mix didn't work, the follow-me-
powder. Her connaissance was as strong as mine.

Zozo Labrique lit a corncob pipe. She wore a full skirt
and a bandana on her head. Her face was black wrinkled
and hard. The sun suddenly appeared, causing the gold
hoops on her ears to sparkle.

Jake the Barker rode up alongside the wagon.

Well Loop, Zozo, won't be long now. Maybe thirty minutes before we pull into Yellow Back Radio. We're
booked by some guy named Happy Times, who we're to
meet at the Hotel.

Jake rode down the mountain's path to advise the rest of
the troupe.

This was a pretty good season Loop, what are you going
to do with your roll?

O I don't know Zozo, maybe I'll hire some bounty hunters
to put a claim on my lost territory.

O Loop quit your joking.

What are you going to do Zozo?

Think the old bag will head back to New Orleans, mecca
of Black America. First Doc John kicked out then me—

she got her cronies in City Hall to close down my opera-
tion. We had to go underground. Things started to
disappear from my humfo—even Henry my snake and
mummies appeared in the curtains. She warned my
clients that if they visited me she'd cross them. Everybody got shook and stayed away. Finally she layed a
trick on me so strong that it almost wasted old Zozo,
Loop. That Marie is a mess. Seems now though my old
arch enemy is about to die. Rumor has it that the daughter is going to take over but I know nothing will come of
that fast gal. Nobody but Marie has the type of connaissance to make men get down on their knees and
howl like dogs and women to throw back their heads
and cackle. Well . . . maybe your old lady, Loop, what's
the hussy's name?

Diane, Black Diane, Zozo, you know her name.

Sometimes it's hard to tell, Loop, the bitch has so many
aliases.

Before their wagon rounded the mountain curve they
heard a gasp go up on the other side. A dead man was
hanging upside down from a tree. He had been shot.

He wore a frilled ruffled collar knee britches a fancy shirt
and turned up shoes. A cone shaped hat with a carnation
on its rim had fallen to the ground.

The two climbed down from the wagon and walked to
where Jake the Barker and the Juggler were staring at
the hanging man. The dancing Bear watched from his
cage, his paws gripping the bars, his head swinging from

side to side with curiosity. Handbills which had dropped from the man's pockets littered the ground about the scene.

Plug In Your Head
Look Here Citizens!!
Coming to Yellow Back Radio
Jake the Barker's lecture room
New Orleans Hoodooine Zozo Labrique
Amazing Loop Garoo lariat tricks
Dancing Bear and Juggler too
Free   Beer

Above the man's head on the hoodoo rock fat nasty buzzards were arriving. Jake removed his hat and was surrounded by members of the bewildered troupe.

Nearest town Video Junction is about fifty miles away. There's not enough grub in the chuck wagon to supply us for a journey of that length. Besides the horses and oxen have to be bedded down. I wouldn't want any of you to take risks. If this means danger up ahead maybe we should disband here, split the take and put everybody on his own.

We've come this far Jake, may as well go on into Yellow Back Radio, the Juggler said.

Count me in too, Loop said, we've braved alkali, coyotes, wolves, rattlesnakes, catamounts, hunters. Nothing I'm sure could be as fierce down in that town—why it even looks peaceful from here.

I'll go along with the rest, Zozo said. But I have a funny feeling that everything isn't all right down there.

After burying the advance man on a slope they rode farther down the mountain until finally, from a vantage point, they could see the rest of Yellow Back Radio.

The wooden buildings stood in the shadows. The Jail House, the Hat and Boot store the Hardware store the Hotel and Big Lizzy's Rabid Black Cougar Saloon.

Sinister hogs with iron jaws were fenced in behind the scaffold standing in the square. They were the swine of the notorious Hangman, who was such a connoisseur of his trade he kept up with all the latest techniques of murder.

A new device stood on the platform. Imported from France, it was said to be as rational as their recent revolution. The hogs ate the remains of those unfortunate enough to climb the platform. Human heads were particularly delectable to these strange beasts.

The troupe drove through the deserted main street of the town. Suddenly they were surrounded by children dressed in the attire of the Plains Indians. It appeared as if cows had been shucked and their skins passed to the children's nakedness for their shoes and clothes were made of the animals' hides.

Reach for the sky, whiskey drinkers, a little spokesman warned. One hundred flintlocks were aimed at them.

Hey it's a circus, one of the children cried, and some dropped their rifles and began to dance.

A circus? one of the boys who made the warning asked.

How do we know this isn't a trap sprung by the cheating old of Yellow Back Radio?

Jake the Barker, holding up his hands, looked around to the other members of the troupe. Amused, Loop, Zozo and the Juggler complied with the little gunmen's request.

What's going on here? Jake asked. We're the circus that travels around this territory each season. We're supposed to end the tour in your town. We're invited by Mister Happy Times. We're to meet him at the Hotel. Where are the adults? The Marshal, the Doctor, the Preacher, or someone in charge?

Some of the children snickered, but became silent when their spokesman called them into a huddle. After some haggling, he stepped towards the lead wagon upon which Jake the Barker rode.

We chased them out of town. We were tired of them ordering us around. They worked us day and night in the mines, made us herd animals harvest the crops and for three hours a day we went to school to hear teachers praise the old. Made us learn facts by rote. Lies really bent upon making us behave. We decided to create our own fiction.

One day we found these pearl-shaped pills in a cave of a mountain. They're what people ages ago called devil's pills. We put them in the streams so that when the grown-ups went to fill their buckets they swallowed some. It confused them more than they were so we moved on them and chased them out of town. Good riddance. They

listened to this old Woman on the talk show who filled
their heads with rot. She was against joy and life the
decrepit bag of sticks, and she put them into the same
mood. They always demanded we march and fight
heathens.

Where are the old people now? Jake asked.

They're camped out at Drag Gibson's spread. We think
they're preparing to launch some kind of invasion but
we're ready for them. Drag just sent his herd up the
Chisholm to market yesterday but there are enough cowpokes left behind to give us a good fight. Our Indian
informant out at Drag's spread tells us the townspeople
haven't given in to Drag's conditions yet. He wants them
to sign over all of their property in exchange for lending
his men to drive us out.

Then he will not only rule his spread which is as large as
Venezuela but the whole town as well. He's the richest
man in the valley, with prosperous herds, abundant resources and an ego as wide as the Grand Canyon.

This nonsense would never happen in the Seven Cities
of Cibola, Jake the Barker said.

The Seven Cities of Cibola? the children asked, moving
in closer to Jake's wagon.

Inanimate things, computers do the work, feed the fowl,
and programmed cows give cartons of milkshakes in 26
flavors.

Yippppeeeeee, the children yelled. Where is it?

It's as far as you can see from where you're standing now. I'm going to search for it as soon as the show is over here but since there is no sponsor to greet us we may as well disband now, Jake said, looking about at the other members of the troupe.

Why don't you entertain us? the children asked.

It's a plot. We decided that we wouldn't trust anybody greying about the temples anymore!

O don't be paranoid, silly, another child replied to the tiny skeptic. Always trying to be the leader just like those old people we ran into the hills. These aren't ordinary old people they're children like us—look at their costumes and their faces.

Let's have the circus, a cry went up.

Well I don't know—you see we have no leaders holy men or gurus either so I'd have to ask the rest of the troupe.

Loop, Zozo and the Juggler said yes by nodding their heads. The Bear jumped up and down in his chains.

Delighted, the children escorted the small circus group to the outskirts of Yellow Back Radio where they pitched the tents, bedded down the weary horses and oxen and made preparations for the show.

● ○

Three horsemen—the Banker, the Marshal and the Doctor—decided to pay a little visit to Drag Gibson's ranch. They had to wait because Drag was at his usual hobby, embracing his property.

A green mustang had been led out of its stall. It served as a symbol for his streams of fish, his herds, his fruit so large they weighed down the mountains, black gold and diamonds which lay in untapped fields, and his barnyard overflowing with robust and erotic fowl.

Holding their Stetsons in their hands the delegation looked on as Drag prepared to kiss his holdings. The ranch hands dragged the animal from his compartment towards the front of the Big Black House where Drag bent over and french kissed the animal between his teeth, licking the slaver from around the horse's gums.

This was one lonely horse. The male horses avoided him because they thought him stuck-up and the females because they thought that since green he was a queer horse. See, he had turned green from old nightmares.

After the ceremony the unfortunate critter was led back to his stall, a hoof covering his eye.

Drag removed a tube from his pocket and applied it to his lips. He then led the men to a table set up in front of the House. Four bottles of whiskey were placed on the table by Drag's faithful Chinese servant, who picked a stray louse from Drag's fur coat only to put it down the cattleman's back. Drag smiled and twitched a bit, slapping his back until his hand found the bullseye. Killing the pest, he and the servant exchanged grins.

Bewildered, the men glanced at each other.

What brings you here? I told you to come only if you were ready for business. Sign the town and your property over to me so that my quest for power will be satisfied. If you do that I'll have my men go in there and wipe them menaces out.

We decided to give in, Drag. Why, we're losing money each day the children hold the town and we have to be around our wives all the time and they call us stupid jerks, buster lamebrain and unpolite things like that. It's a bargain, Drag. What do we do now?

Now you're talking business Doc. Sign this stiffycate which gives me what I asked for and I'll have them scamps out of your hair in no time.

Drag brought forth an official looking document from inside his robe, to which the Banker, Marshal and Doctor affixed their signatures.

It's a good thing we got the people to see it your way, the Banker said, wiping the sweat on his forehead with a crimson handkerchief. Some reinforcements were arriving today. They were in some wagons that was painted real weird and we hanged and shot one who was dressed like a clown. We thought they might be heathens from up North, you dig?

You mulish goofies, that was the circus I ordered to divert the kids so's we could ambush them. Any damned fool knows kids like circuses.

Drag we're confused and nervous. Just today four boxes of drexol were stolen from our already dwindling supply of goods. That's why we didn't think when we killed that man. The old people are wandering around the camp bumping into each other they're so tightened up. All day people are saying hey stupid idiot watch where you're going. It's a mad house.

And the Preacher Rev. Boyd, he's in the dumps in a strong and serious way this time. You know how hard he tried with the kids and the town's heathen, how he'd smoke hookahs with them brats and get stoned with Chief Showcase the only surviving injun and that volume of hip pastorale poetry he's putting together, *Stomp Me O Lord.* He thought that Protestantism would survive at least another month and he's tearing up the Red-Eye and writing more of them poems trying to keep up with the times. Drag you know how out of focus things are around here. After all Drag it's your world completely now.

How can you be so confident your men can take care of them varmits Drag? It takes a trail boss a dozen or so cowboys and a wrangler to get the herd North. You can't have many cowpokes left behind. Don't get me wrong I'm not afraid for myself cause I rode with Doc Holiday and the Dalton Boys before I went peace officer—I have handled a whole slew of punks passing through the hopper in my day . . . why if I hadn't been up the creek at the Law Enforcement Conference it wouldn't have happened anyway.

You always seem to be at some convention when the town needs you Marshal, Drag said, looking into a hand

mirror and with a neckerchief wiping the smudges of
mascara that showed above his batting lashes.

Drag, the women folk, well you know how women are,
what strange creatures they be during menopause.
They're against us wiping out the kids. That's one of the
reasons we didn't cast lots quicker to give you the hand
over of Yellow Back Radio, so that you could adjust all
the knobs and turn to whatever station you wished. Anyway we tried to get Big Lizzy to talk to them but they
don't recognize her as one of their own.

Pshaw, don't worry about the women Doc, Drag Gibson
said, bringing his old fat and ugly frame to its feet. Start
appeasing them and pretty soon they'll be trying to run
the whole show like that kook back in Wichita who cam-
paigned to cut out likker. Now quit your whining and
get back to camp and see after them townsfolk. Leave
the job up to me.

The dignitaries rose and tumbled down the hill. The
Banker rolled over a couple of times as Drag stood jerk-
ing his shoulders and with one finger in his ear as pellet
after pellet flew over the Marshal's, Banker's and Doctor's heads. He relaxed, drank a glass of rotgut and gave
the appearance of a statesman by returning to his book
The Life of Catherine the Great. As soon as the delegation disappeared, he slammed the book shut and called
his boys.

Get in here cowpokes, we're in business.

Skinny McCullough the foreman followed by some cowhands rushed onto the lawn and surrounded their boss.

Chinaboy! Chinaboy! Bring me that there package.

The Chinese servant rushed into the scene with his arms weighed down with a bundle.

O.K. men, Drag said, this is the opportunity we've been waiting for. They signed the town over to me, the chumps, haw haw.

He opened the package and placed its contents on the table.

This is a brand new revolving cylinder. It has eight chambers. A murderer's dream with a rapid firing breech-loading firearm.

The cowpokes' eyes lit up and foam began to form around their lips.

It was invented by a nice gent lecturer named Dr. Coult of New York London and Calcutta. Just bought it from Royal Flush Gooseman, the shrewd, cunning and wicked fur trapper, the one who sold them injuns those defected flintlocks allowing us to wipe them out.

The kids are down there with a circus I booked under a pseudonym. I been watching them through my long glass. Now get busy and before you know it Drag Gibson will be the big name in Yellow Back Radio then Video Junction then va-va-voom on to the East, heh heh heh.

The cowpokes from Drag Gibson's Purple Bar-B drank some two-bits-a-throw from a common horn and armed

with their shiny new weapons headed towards the outskirts of Yellow Back Radio on their nefarious mission.

● ○

The Dancing Bear, the Juggler, Loop and Zozo entertained the children far into the night. The Dancing Bear
did acrobatic feats with great deftness, Loop his loco
lariat tricks, and Zozo read the children's palms and told
their fortunes.

Finally Jake the Barker gathered them near the fire to
tell of the Seven Cities of Cibola, magnificent legendary
American paradise where tranquilized and smiling machines gladly did all of the work so that man could be
free to dream. A paradise whose streets were paved with
opals from Idaho, sapphire from Montana, turquoise and
silver from the great Southwest:

In the early half of the sixteenth century about 1528 an
expedition which included the black slave Estevancio
landed at Tampa Bay. He and his companions were lost
trapped and enslaved by Indians. Other expeditions also
vanished mysteriously. Legend has it that the city can
only be found by those of innocent motives, the young
without yellow fever in their eyes.

Stupid historians who are hired by the cattlemen to pro-
mote reason, law and order—toad men who adore facts
—say that such an anarchotechnological paradise where
robots feed information into inanimate steer and mechanical fowl where machines do everything from dig

irrigation ditches to mine the food of the sea help old ladies across the street and nurture infants is as real as a green horse's nightmare. Shucks I've always been a fool, eros appeals more to me than logos. I'm just silly enough to strike out for it tomorrow as soon as the circus splits up.

A place without gurus monarchs leaders cops tax collectors jails matriarchs patriarchs and all the other galoots who in cahoots have made the earth a pile of human bones under the feet of wolves.

Why don't we all go, the children shrieked.

Wait a minute, Jake said, we don't have enough supplies for the trip. It lies somewhere far to the south.

That's no task, supplies, one of the children said.

After huddling together they all started into the town, leaving the troupe behind. Finally having had a loot-in on the Hat and Boot store, the Feed store and the Bank they returned with enough supplies to make the long journey.

I guess I can't argue against that, Jake said turning to Loop, Zozo and the Juggler. Welcome to my expedition into the unknown.

The children reveled and danced around.

When they finished storing provisions into the wagons the entire party went to sleep. The next morning there would be much work to do. The troupe bedded down in their wagons and the children slept beneath warm buffalo robes.

● ○

Loop Garoo was dreaming of bringing down the stars with his tail when all at once he smelled smoke. He awoke to find horsemen surrounding the circle. The children began to scream and some of their clothes caught fire from torches the bandits had tossed into the area. Rapid gunfire started up and the children fell upon each other and ran about in circles as they tried to break the seizure's grip. Zozo Labrique looked out of her wagon and was shot between the eyes. She dropped to the ground next to the wagon. The pitiful moans of the children could be heard above the din of hoofbeats and gunfire as one by one they were picked off by horsemen who fired with amazing accuracy. The Juggler was firing two rifles and before catching a bullet in his throat was able to down two of the horsemen.

Loop crawled to the place where Zozo lay dying. Blood trickled from her nose and mouth.

Zozo let me see if I can get you inside your wagon.

Flee boy, save yourself, I'm done for, the woman murmured pressing something into his hand. It's a mad dog's tooth it'll bring you connaissance and don't forget the gris gris, the mojo, the wangols old Zozo taught you and when you need more power play poker with the dead.

But Zozo I'll try to get you a horse, Loop began—but with a start the woman slumped in his arms.

The grizzly Bear had escaped from the cage and was mangling two horsemen. This allowed an opening in the circle which two children raced through, hanging from the sides of horses. Loop did likewise but so as to divert the men from the children rode in a different direction, towards the desert.

Bullet after bullet zitted above his head. When the burning scene of children and carny freaks was almost out of his sight he looked back. His friends the Juggler, a dancing bear, the fast talking Barker and Zozo Labrique were trapped in a deadly circle. Their figurines were beginning to melt.

II. The Loop Garoo Kid Comes Back Mad

In Bath County, Kentucky in 1876, several tons of dried beef fell from the sky. How did this mass of meat get up into the sky—and how specifically dried beef?

from "The Day It Rained Cows"
Ronald J. Willis,
East Village Other, March 1st, 1968

Roy Rogers' movie double's name was Whitey Christensen.

from *New York Journal American*
Col. 5, May 4, 1948

Loop Garoo had to shoot his hoss. He hated to do it but under the circumstances it turned out to be the wisest thing he could do. The horse was a snafu anyway. One of Drag Gibson's gunmen had wounded the animal in the leg.

You ever see a horse shot in the movies? So that gives you an idea of the fluke of luck Loop was reeling in on this queer fish of a day. First his gun burned down and now a lame horse. All around as far as one could see— desert. A hot mean and bitchy desert with a naturally formed misanthropic mood seemed to be saying well Loop good buddy, how you want it dished up, scorpion bite, rattlesnake, order anything you see, it seemed to be whispering in the voice of the rude hash slinger of the rockbottom dives of our lives.

Loop, weak and spent, dozed off, his arms stretched out in front of him. In the distance large birds with buzzard coupons could be seen lining up for mess.

He awoke to find himself surrounded by horsemen. The leader of this shabby crew—well they appeared shabby but closer inspection revealed bell bottom denims of a custom-made variety and fancy shirts which must have cost a pretty penny. The scarfs they wore about their necks were of an extravagantly rich material.

If it isn't the alienated individualist stuck out here in the desert, the leader of these grim horsemen said.

It was Bo Shmo and the neo-social realist gang. They rode to this spot from their hideout in the hills. Bo Shmo leaned in his saddle and scowled at Loop, whom he considered a deliberate attempt to be obscure. A buffoon an outsider and frequenter of sideshows.

Bo Shmo was dynamic and charismatic as they say. He made a big reputation in the thirties, not having much originality, by learning to play Hoagland Howard Carmichael's "Buttermilk Sky" backwards. He banged the piano and even introduced some novel variations such as sliding his rump across the black and whites for that certain affect.   piano ✱

People went for it. It was in all the newspapers. He traveled from coast to coast exhibiting his ass and everything was fine until the real Hoagland Howard Carmichael (the real one) showed up and went for Bo Shmo's goat. He called him a lowdown patent thief and railed him out of town. You would think that finding themselves duped, the imposter's fans would demand his hide. Not so, Americans love being conned if you can do it in a style that is both grand and entertaining. Consider P. T. Barnum's success, Semple McPherson and other notables. A guy who rigs aluminum prices can get himself introduced by Georgie Jessel at 100 dollars a plate but stealing a can of beer can get you iced.

So sympathetic Americans sent funds to Bo Shmo which he used to build one huge neo-social realist Institution in the Mountains. Wagon trains of neo-social realist composers writers and painters could be seen winding up its path.

Hey Bo, one of his sidekicks spoke up. We'd better blast this guy right off the way I look at it. Nobody will miss him since he went out with that carnival. If he makes it across the desert he might land a typewriter and do a book on his trials. He'll corner the misery market and pound out one of those Christian confessionals to which we are so much endeared. Then where will we be. How will we buy all these campy cowboy suits . . .

Shut up, Bo said slapping the man in the face with his prospector's cap. The other horsemen remained mute. Bo Shmo did all their thinking for them. Their job was merely to fold their arms and look mean at the hoe-downs or rather the shakedowns. You see Bo Shmo was a real collectivist. Worked hard at it. Fifty toothbrushes cluttered his bathroom and when he walked down the street it seemed a dozen centipedes headed your way. He woke up in the morning with crowds and went to bed with a mob. The man loved company. It seemed that he wore people under his coat although none of them would pull it for him. He resembled Harpo Marx at times, you know, the scene where Harpo has shoplifted a market and stuffed all the smoked hams under an oversized coat. He looked like that.

individualism

The trouble with you Loop is that you're too abstract, the part time autocrat monarchist and guru finally said. Crazy dada nigger that's what you are. You are given to fantasy and are off in matters of detail. Far out esoteric bullshit is where you're at. Why in those suffering books that I write about my old neighborhood and how hard it was every gumdrop machine is in place while your work is a blur and a doodle. I'll bet you can't create the difference between a German and a redskin. ?

What's your beef with me Bo Shmo, what if I write circuses? No one says a novel has to be one thing. It can be anything it wants to be, a vaudeville show, the six o'clock news, the mumblings of wild men saddled by demons.

All art must be for the end of liberating the masses. A landscape is only good when it shows the oppressor hanging from a tree. communism

Right on! Right on, Bo, the henchmen chorused.

Did you receive that in a vision or was it revealed to you?

Look out now Loop don't get quippy with me, I'll have one of my men take you off. We can't afford the luxury of individualism gumming up our rustling. We blast those who don't agree with us.

Aw leave me alone Bo Shmo to doing my thing which for now is dying. You presume to be able to give other people decrees—living in your expensive neo-social realist retreat while commonfolk who follow your rants try to match their nickel plates with aeroplanes and tanks. One of these days those people are going to rise up from the pavement where they died clutching coupons and unredeemable refuse from shop windows and take it out on your hide.

O.K. fat mouth, you asked for it. Discipline him fellows.

The horsemen dismounted and began to put Loop through changes. Being neo-social realist and not very original they gave him a version of Arab Death. They smeared jelly on his face and buried him up to the neck in desert. Soon his face would be crawling with vermin which was certainly no picnic of a way to go.

Suddenly above them a whirring noise.

Gads! Bo said, the arch-nemesis of villains like me. The Flying Brush Beeve Monster. Let's get out of here.

The horsemen mounted their nags and with Bo Shmo out front headed back to their institution in the mountains.

Not only would he be a desert carrion, but now something right out of Science Fiction was descending upon him from the heavens, Loop thought. It resembled a monster insect whatever it was and when it landed it stirred up the sand so that Loop couldn't make out its dimensions. Much to his surprise a plainclothes Indian casually stepped out of the monster's belly. He held a cigarette holder in his hand. He strode to the position where Loop'd been tied down in the sand and lifted a canteen to the outlaw's lips.

Champagne! Who are you?

Never mind my man, I was on the way to Europe for an appointment with my tailor when I happened upon you surrounded by those mediocre bandits. The desert was fine until they moved into those hills coming out of their fancy hideout only to make raids on sniveling and s/m liberals that take that sick tour.

What tour?

O there's this Royal Flush Gooseman, a rattlesnake heart if there ever was, he hires wagon trains which bring liberals out here for the purpose of having the trains surrounded by Bo Shmo and his henchmen. The whole thing is staged if you ask me. Since my people are no longer around to raise war parties Bo Shmo and his men are taking all the loot. Deserts are for visions not for materialists. Read any American narrative about crossing—apparitions, ravens walking about as tall as men, the whole goldern phantasmagoria. Maybe I can give you a lift to Video Junction, the town lying about 50 miles from here?

Loop regarded the Monster with apprehension.

O don't worry about that. I created it to get around in, made it from spare parts I found in deserted ghost towns. I also used a new kind of plant called plastic I discovered growing in the hills like wildfire.

I'm a kind of patarealist Indian going about inventing do dads. This machine comes in better than nags and creaky stagecoaches. Stupid shmucks and boobs around here think it's some kind of flying ghost cow. Legends, whispering among the peasants, protective charms on the door of each house. The whole bit. Bo Shmo and the cattlemen are in the same routine. Afraid of anything that can get off the ground, materialists that they are—anything capable of groovy up up and aways strikes terror in their hearts.

The Indian freed Loop and escorted him to his hobby lying in the sand.

I call it a helicopter, lots of mileage on very little fuel, but I wouldn't be surprised if bad medicine steals the patents and calls them his own. Honkie. Devil.

Loop smiled.

John D. Rockefeller didn't have an original idea in his life and George Gershwin stole pillows from sleeping Negroes plush vampire that he was and where did you think Mae West got her manic depressive female swishing? In New York City as you read me now some woman done took Martha and the Vandellas "Dancing In The Streets" and calls it her very own.

You listen to Soul Music, Chief?

Sure man; all the time, the Indian replied releasing the wheel of the helicopter and breaking into a strong boogaloo from the waist up. The craft rocked.

I don't even want to go into how Moses sneaked around the Pharaoh's court abusing this hospitality by swiping all the magic he could get his clutches around. If I run down that shit, Loop, the book won't be reviewed in Manhattan . . . and look what the Fiend did to us. We showed the cat how to ride, what to wear, how to plant, woodcraft, how to tan, tried to teach them riding bareback but they were so repressed they had to use a saddle, and on Friday nights we introduced a new recreation for these dull creatures.

What was that?

Taught them to pop corn and when you got that popcorn covered with maple syrup you got crackerjacks. Man they didn't know from dick. We gave them all those things and you know what we got in return?

What?

Liquor smallpox and guns. Well, Royal Flush Gooseman came through and sold our tribe some defective rifles and that was the end.

How did you escape?

I was away spearing salmon. You see the tribe was so busy trying to organize they forgot that they were clandestine by nature, camouflage, now you see now you don't, what some blockheads call esoteric bullshit. But now I'm trying the same thing on him he put us through.

What was that?

Foment mischief among his tribes and they will destroy each other. Not only that. I have my secret weapon.

O, said Loop yawning.

The Chief Showcase revealed a pipe. He put some tobacco in its bowl.

If I can't get their scalps I'll get their lungs. My fellow tribesmen, I told them we were outnumbered, but they were in a meat thing, rushing like the buffalo over cliffs to certain disaster. You think I wanted to end up in front of a barber shop with a tomahawk in one hand and box of cigars in the other or have my face printed on a nickel? No, this time it'll be done by an idea, not toying around with gumshoes.

What handle do you go by Chief?

Chief Showcase.

Chief Showcase, Loop thought, remembering the Indian names he'd heard like Toohoolhoolzote, Looking Glass, and Man-Afraid-Of-His-Horse which opened up new possibilities of being named after phobias, objects or even words that didn't mean anything but sounded like music.

I know what you're thinking Loop. You're thinking that from all of the beautiful Indian names, Chief Showcase is kind of a letdown. I assure you it works though. You see, I'm Chief Cochise's cousin so that makes me Chief Showcase. Yuk yuk yuk.

The helicopter sped on its journey.

I don't want to take you out of your way Indian.

No sweat, the Chief replied, I'm sure my accountant can come up with something like "entertaining the Great Meshuga," Chief Showcase winked at Loop.

You have heap bit gnosis to be such a young man and only to have lived one life. The Loop smiled sadly.

I recognized you right away, O Morning Star. Besides, Indians and black people have been roaming the plains of America together for hundreds of years. Why one of the chiefs of my tribe, the Crow, was James P. Beckwith, and Dick Gregory represented our Washington tribes in their treaty fights. Knappy hair rises like grass from the tracks through the Mandans and the Arikaras made by Sgt. York. And the Seminole fought invasion after invasion against the Fiend to protect black fugitive slaves. Take a look inside that compartment, the Chief said, pointing to one of the panels with one hand and steering the copter with the other.

Loop opened the door to see a plate of steaming chitterlings with potato salad on the side, collard greens, and a champagne bottle wrapped in a towel immersed in a bucket of ice.

What you might call Soul D Luxe, hey Loop? The Indian whistled cheerfully.

Loop finished his supper and leaned back. He thought malicious thoughts. He would woodshed. He would follow Zozo Labrique's instructions to the T.

You know, Loop, we Crows are called the Beau Brummels of the Indians, so in order to show that my attributes are contagious I'm going to give you this credit card to one of the finest stores in Video Junction. Bet you'd look good in black buckskin with pink fringes.

O come on Chief you've done enough already.

No take it Loop, get yourself refreshed, and there's an

occult bookstore around the corner from the Hotel. It's a bodega front and they sell John the Conquerer roots and rattlesnake vertebrae.

Well Chief if you insist, but if I ever sell this mind sauna to Hollywood I'll give you all of Gene Autry's bicycles.

How did you like that champagne Loop? It was made by a friend of mine in the mountains. California grapes no less. Get to that. I'll bet they'll be as in as this helicopter or French vintage a 100 years from now.

The Flying Brush Beeve tolled its way across the sky. Loop didn't hear the Chief's last one liner. He was musing. In his dreams Loop scribbled on a postcard a note to an old friend.

> *Dear Joy. This time the*
> *Witches win. Love*
> *Loop Garoo*

Ahead the lines of Video Junction moved in.

● ○

The other cowhands, unable to save their comrades who had been mauled by the burning Bear, rode back to the Purple Bar-B to report to Drag Gibson. Drag sat on a black velvet couch, his belly peeking out over his waist as if to say hello through its tiny red mouth of a navel. His reading of *Catherine* was interrupted by the jingle of guthooks mounting the steps of the Purple Bar-B's Big Black House.

Well boss we took care of them hard boppers who were camped outside the town. Only 4 casualties. One of the hands was eaten by a grizzly and some of the brains spattered our clothes, tasted something like veal. And there was this Juggler who shot so fast the stars abandoned their heavenly places to become his spectators but we plugged him too.

Good, Drag said sticking a pudgy pink hand into the pocket of his monogrammed silk robe recently ordered from St. Louis.

Gee Drag something stinks in here—phew. It's worse than the smell out there in camp where the circus lies in smoking ruins. Like the smell of tallow my ma use to burn for soap—like death, Drag.

Drag tapped the table next to the sofa while his eyes innocently scanned the ceiling.

Wonder what it could be boys? Go over and get Preacher Boyd to walk around with his hazel wand so's the women'll be satisfied. You know how women folk are. They love rhythm and ritual. Shuts them up all the time. Few flowers and a handful of shiny minerals, those crosses we left on Normandy beaches all tidy and in a neat row a couple of horns doing taps. Hell, their whole bodies are drawn by the goddamn moon. It plays upon their hides as it does the tides. Can't help themselves. Telegram from the War Department sung at the door, couple of guys folding flags they'll forget all about them punks. Another generation they'll be sending more out to get slaughtered. All you have to do is say Mother Country play upon their vanity.

Glad you got rid of them hooligans boys, they didn't like to march and was lazy. Talked about love and such things which is mush, right boys?

Mush is right, Skinny answered as he and two cowhands, as if to emphasize Drag's remarks, ran their hands across their lips and spat out repulsive and invisible kisses.

I don't know if Preacher Rev. Boyd will work out this time Drag, last time we saw him it was when the forces of the old recaptured Big Lizzy's Rabid Black Cougar Saloon. He started to have d.t.'s and said something about a gila monster who was God.

Those Protestants, so lazy with allegory.

What did you say boss?

Nothing boys, just a blue streak inflaming my mind, it'll go away.

Anyway boss you'd better see after him now. Whenever he uses that stick only dogs of Yellow Back Radio gather about to watch. Others poke fun and prod.

Drag thought a minute then snapped his fingers making a flat blubbery thick.

When State Magic fails unofficial magicians become stronger

Somebody say something? What was that? Did you say something foreman Skinny McCullough, one of you cowpokes say something?

No Drag, Skinny said shaking in his boots and spurs.

Drag looked around the ceiling again. He stared at the open window. Tiny black fingers were crawling over the sill. Drag drew his six shooter and fired into the night. The men climbed back from beneath the furniture where they had hid during the unexpected gunplay.

Boss, Skinny cried, what's wrong with you?

Thought I saw some hands at the window.

Drag's breathing became rapid. Sweat poured down his cheeks. He placed the smoking gun on the table.

Anyway boys, good work. Why don't you go over to Big Lizzy's Rabid Black Cougar and have one on me. Paint Yellow Back Radio red. You've done a good job. No more furious aggressive wiggles of them kids and the clown show closed down too. Can't say we were humorless—let them go out with a carny. Har har.

Well not exactly boss, Skinny said, two of them kids escaped and the Loop Garoo Kid from the circus rode off towards the town fifty miles from here. He seemed to be savage mad.

He'll never make it—across those cow skulls, cactus, rattle-snakes, stinging lizards, vinegarroon, cougars and whatever heathen lies out there now that we got rid of them injuns—speaking of injuns how did them Coult rifles work for you?

They're good for us boss—we're going to really get rid of the next heathen that raises his feather from behind the rock.

Too bad you let them escape though—sometimes I think I'm short of the genuine article around here boys.

Boss we tried to get em but never seed no hombre ride off like that—he was fastern a souped-up hare. Don't worry boss if he shows his face in Yellow Back Radio, if indeed he manages to through some miracle escape—if lowly desert vermin don't get him the Flying Brush Beeve will. As for the kids they're done for before they started. They headed for this unexplored territory to the south. Some kind of heathen co-operative society down there too. They'll be eaten or boiled in a caldron.

Now get, boys, so's I can be alone with my thoughts which is a pretty spooky situation since Drag is not only nickname for the horseman who rides to the rear of the herd catching the dust, bringing up the stragglers and sick among the cattle but my name is also shorthand for something scaly, slimy and huge with dirt.

Gee Drag it's great to have a smooth talking white man like you leading us you must get all that information from the book you're always reading, Skinny McCullough said as he and the ebullient cowhands departed for Yellow Back Radio.

● ○

*Just suppose that the Loop Garoo Kid managed to get
through all the tests waiting for him between Yellow
Back Radio and the town lying fifty miles from here. He'll
come after me. You know, the revenge motif. What the
hell may as well make hay while the sun shines. Take my
wife for an instant. Black cows donated their organs,
orphans, widow women, squatters and sheep herders donated their teeth I stole eyeballs kidneys livers from road
agents and injuns all stored down in the basement. What
a mess. Still she's getting worse. Anyway what did the
old Woman on the talk show say, "I suggested the sits
bath and herbs to make her last months comfortable Drag
my darling listener. Truth is she will die off shortly like
some great red hog who has swallowed tacks, she will
end up on Forty-second Street a pale reminder of a
government inspected hotdog." Here I am, old, ugly,
mean and ignorant. Fish fill my lakes as if they were
spawnings paradise my barnyard overflows with the
pecking order of erotic cocks. My fruit is so plentiful
their orchards weigh down the valley. Black diamonds,
black gold and other precious minerals lie in great untapped beds so huge they would dwarf even my ego.
And about 3000 head started up the Chisholm to market
yesterday. But what would happen if I popped off like
the rest of the swells what's pushing up daisies out in the
bone orchard?*

*The old Woman told us chances are 1–65,000 poker odds
that a new crop of kids would come on the scene pro-*

*testing, having love feasts and trying to turn the town
into an open city. What I gotta do is start the flow towards
docility a-gushing. Get rid of this broken seed stored in
my loins. It aches. I will have some nice obedient progeny
who will manage all the forms after I'm gone and nickel-
odeon for the worms.*

*What am I waitin for? I got to knock off that horrible
hybrid in the kitchen and take a swell looking art nou-
veau broad.* But before he could act he looked around. It
was like a monster flickah drammer—the confrontation.
Horrible hybrid meets Spooky Situation. Horrible hybrid
was dripping wet. She walked across the room on her
leafy feet webbed hands outstretched and the scales of
horrible hybrid's body shown green by the kerosene lamp.

In a quivering voice the Various Arrangement of Dead
Parts said: What happened Drag dear husband you were
supposed to bring me a towel?

Spooky Situation removed the six shooter from his holster
and emptied it into Horrible Hybrid but the junk kept
coming, sloshing across the floor to embrace Drag.

Drag managed to get over to the gun rack. There he
picked out a Winchester and fired ball after ball into the
creature's chest until it made some unusual groan and
dropped to the floor.

Chinaboy, Chinaboy. Come in here will you? The chinaboy ran into the room. His slanted eyes became orbs and
he threw up his small yellow hands when he saw whatever it was lying on the floor.

Mop this up and bury it on the hillside. Crops looked a little weak up there this year, Drag said pointing to the bubbling mass on the rug and spitting tobacco on his wife's remains. Drag hobbled over to the fireplace. He threw some pieces which lay on the floor into the fire, ran his hands across the sticky yellow patch of bull's sperm on his head and put on a dressing gown. The Great House was empty except for Drag.

Guess I'll go upstairs now and burn the marriage stiffy-cate, Drag thought, climbing into the portable elevator attached to the side of the winding staircase. He ascended to the second story of the building.

Once upstairs Drag removed the marriage certificate from the wall and put it into the fire. He then sat down and drank some whiskey.

Suddenly something black jumped out of the closet, leaped through the window into the yard. What the? Drag thought, a cigar falling from his lips and onto the floor.

● ○

At Big Lizzy's Rabid Black Cougar, Drag was being discussed in earnest by the foreman and two cowhands from his ranch.

A daffy cat a really daffy cat, started saying spooky things about magic.

The foreman stared at the plump pink of nude dangling a flower between her teeth painted in an oil portrait above two moose horns hanging behind the bar.

Those kids said some nasty things about the six gun, the foreman addressed the bartender. Said we ought to unzip our pants and draw it from there. Them smart alecks good riddance.

Just then a tall mustached man walked into the bar. He wore a slouch hat single breasted black frock coat and flowing black tie. A star rested near his right breast.

Boys, the Marshal said, putting a hand on Skinny's shoulders, thought you might want to know that the middle aged of Yellow Back Radio voted to commend you for saving the town from them kids who had it under siege. Didn't even need the Preacher and his hazel wand this time. Just talked fast and said freedom every three words. They said they were grateful to you and the boys for freeing Yellow Back Radio from the kids. They're glad you got rid of those brats who were being influenced with Spirit. Everybody take their hats off.

The bartender removed his Straw, the Marshal his Slouch and the foreman his Stetson and the cowpokes seated at the tables their battered and beat up Ten Gallons.

The Preacher Rev. Boyd, who was down at the other end of the bar, kept still. He was crying into his beer. Tears covered the froth of the stein.

I did everything, sponsored light shows, took them off

the streets and nothing worked. O what am I going to
do? What the Church lacked in aesthetic it couldn't even
make up in pyrotechnics.

The Marshal and foreman and the bartender winked all
around as the Preacher turned a greedy trembling hand
up to his lips and drank down the two bits a throw of
Red-Eye whiskey.

What's going on tonight boys?

There's a lecture room over at the Hotel, Marshal, Skinny
said. Got some bandits' heads in jars preserved in alcohol
—we saw it last night. It was good and nasty, not like a
necktie party which at best gives only a few epiphanous
and titillating moments but long, sustained. Eyes were
bulging and we stood there with our glimmers hypno-
tized like the jars were a pair of rep-towls. The faces were
wet and covered with a red silky substance. It was better than that dog fight where the one hound ate into the
other pooch's maw. But not as good as those scalps belonging to one hundred injun children and squaws that
they exhibited last week.

Outside it began to rain on the rooftops of the Hat and
Boot store, the Feed store. Their tops, reflecting the
heaven's disturbance, went on and off like blue tubes.

Marshal what are you going to do if the Loop Garoo Kid
develops some kind of specialized mystique and comes
hunting for us because we burned down the party? How
are you going to get him shoved into the pokey? Into the
hoosegow? Into the dim, dark sneezers?

No problem, the Marshal said putting a boot on the rail of the bar. Me and Kit Carson use to kill an injun every morning before hoecake and salty dog. He loved violence so we buried him with his shotgun, case he ran into some persnickety spooks beyond the Great Divide. I'm sure I can handle the Kid if he rises from some remote crypt and hangs out horrific super-hero shingles with a side dish of unusual origin process.

Haw haw, Skinny the foreman laughed. Marshal you ain't nothin but an old hoss-eater. How's about a taste of Red-Eye all around.

Where's Big Lizzy, bartender? the Marshal asked.

She's up in the hills hunting for meese.

You mean moose don't you bartender? the Marshal asked.

No, Marshal, meese. Goose is to geese as moose is to meese. I know we're out in the old frontier but everything can't be in a state of anarchy, I mean how will we communicate?

You got a point there, Skinny added, but we cowpokes make up language as we go along. Compare our names for landscape, towns, industry, with those of tenderfoots back East—Syracuse, Troy, Ithaca, not to mention all those towns with names ending in yorks, burghs, villes— they got some inferiority thing back East. Seem to worship Europe. Why there's a whole school in New York of poets writing like Frenchmen. But when you get out here, except for those names given by injuns and Spaniards, cow-

poke genius takes over—Milk River, Hangtown, Poker
Flats, Tombstone, Boot Hill. On and on. I heard that
one of them dudes back there named Webster wants
everybody to speak Hebrew.

Har har, the Marshal said, you can't be for real.

No, Skinny said, I heard it over the radio.

I think maybe he's right Marshal, the barkeep said. One
of them historians remarked at a recent convention that
we're the only Americans or something like that. Said the
real American personality begins with the frontier.

There was silence as the barkeep poured the boys some
brandy on the house.

Big Lizzy said she found a necklace up there in the
mountains—strung together with human teeth—and she
found some odd arrowheads, and fish hooks.

Some kind of injuns we missed, barkeep? the foreman
asked.

We got em all, Skinny. Left old Sitting Bull down at the
Oklahoma Fair selling porny postcards. Must be some
kind of mystery peculiar to Yellow Back Radio. These are
certainly weird times. The old Woman on the talk show
said we shouldn't relax our vigilance one bit—she expects
an invasion any day.

The door swung open and the shotgun messenger from
the Black Swan Stagecoach burst into the room.

Gimmie a drink, gimmie a drink of Red-Nose quick! The man's hands trembled as the shot glass touched his lips.

What's wrong Zeke? the Marshal asked.

He took a long swig then slammed the glass down on the bar. He spoke through an opening in the white hair which covered his face:

Town lying about fifty miles from here—Video Junction. Everybody dead except for the kids up in the mountains dancing and smoking injun tobaccy and some women arriving to a shindig on the backs of obscene goats. Without no floogers on. Nekkid. Was bettern a topless. One of them hookers had knockers on her that was biggern a heliummed grapefruit. Three black cowboys were seated on tree stumps drinking from some wooden bowl and grinning. One of 'em was playing the slide trombone.

Then everybody got on the ground. They was gnashing their teeth and rolling over each other and the air got all hot and funky. Finally they took some woman and put her on a platform on a log, then this one black cowboy took a Bowie and jugged the woman in the chest. She didn't even yell but said some furriner jaw-breaking word, exquisite exquisite, said it over and over again.

We skedaddled out of there fast. And when we reached the Hotel we found dead men everywhere. Dead men in the streets dead men in the rain barrels dead men hanging from lampposts—why the whole town was one big dead. There were little black caskets covered with skulls and crossbones all over the steps of the main buildings.

You sure you wasn't drinking Zeke? the Marshal asked.

No I seed it, I seed it it was awful, the shotgun messenger said, just as the sun went out a trail of razzberry over Yellow Back Radio.

● ○

The Dr. sat across from Drag. He raised his cup to his lips, then spat out the contents. How many times have I told you I take two lumps in my java Chinaboy? he said, biffing the man on the head with his cane.

Chinaboy let loose and splurched the Dr. in the smush.

Take that, you solly looking cleep!

Why you, Dr. said wiping the crust from his face and reaching for his gun. I'm going to plug you, you little varmit.

Haw haw don't let him upset you, Drag consoled, let all the little yellow infidels sass you. I run a democratic household, all the oppressed people, those carrying trays, hog sloppers, cow milkers, fruit pickers and miners are allowed to insult me—like the celebrated nigger dwarf Zip of Barnum Bailey fame. Little minority thought he owned the sideshow and had hired everybody in it. Nobody let him know any better. Longest freak show to run in the history of the circus.

Watch this, Doc, from the talking box, Drag said remov-

ing his princess phone from its cradle and giving it to the
Dr. Listen to this recorded message.

Your world Drag Gibson, definitely your world. The
white man is smarter than God.

Hear that injun, that's my injun.

Chief Cochise's cousin? asked the Dr. dabbing the last
few pieces of crust from his face, tasting some of the
icing on his fingers.

No Chief Cochise's stand-in, Chief Showcase.

Maybe you got something there Drag, maybe I'll try that
on my household staff.

I give him imported hookahs, Pierre Cardin originals,
moccasins decorated with rhinestones, aqua-blue head-
dress, world-wide aeroplane credit.

By the way why did you call me up here Drag?

O routine thing Doc. See that huge damp spot on the rug?
I just bumped off my old lady. I want you to get me a
death stiffycate, you know the Great White Father, or
shall I say the President in the East, is probably getting
jealous of me cause I'm so fine and the top man and all.
They just need an excuse to get the cavalry in here and
start up a grand jury.

Sure Drag that's a simple matter, but don't you think
people are going to get suspicious? That makes the sixth

tomato who's come in with the harvest. Look Drag, you remember that boar we were cooking at last year's corn festival? That boar moved its lips, Drag. The Doc dropped to his knees and weeping, tugged at Drag's pajamas.

Aw Doc you've been hitting the morphine again, said Drag, giving him a go-on wave. You sound like them iggnerant herdsmen, animals talking, omens.

Drag, the Dr. continued, Yellow Back Radio is breaking down. Why Drag, today the sun turned off and the barnyard is going backwards. Geese bark like dogs and feathered horses are a-quacking.

Aw take this towel and honk your snozzle Dr. You've been under pressure or something, right?

The Dr. screamed when he saw the hand roll out from the towel.

The chinee couldn't clean up the last dame thoroughly, the little whippersnapper. I'm going to complain to the agency, Drag said, tossing the hand into the fire, causing a small explosion.

They peeked over the sofa after the smoke had died down.

Wow.

Doc there's nothing wrong with ladykilling. Why I don't need em—I got *Cowboy Mag.* Man, did you see that polled Angus in there last month? Drag said wringing his right hand. Wow. Too much. And when I get tired of it I kiss my green horse.

Well Drag here it is, the Doc said, handing him the certificate.

Dr. walked through the pile of whiskey bottles which turned on their necks and clinked.

Good night Doc, Drag said to his old friend.

Good night Drag, the Doc responded heading towards his buckboard.

The moon was so low Drag felt like reaching over his shoulder and bringing it down and would have too that is had he his back to it but that wouldn't have worked seeing as how he needed his finger tips to scratch the intense itching now covering his body.

● ○

Jeff Williams and Alcibiades Johnson, two horsemen wearing berets with their cowboy costumes, were riding towards the mouth of a cave tucked away in the Blackfoot Mountains not far from Drag's spread. They dismounted and entered. They walked into its depths past stalagmites and other cave furnishings.

Did you get the scarf? Alcibiades asked Jeff.

Yeah man, does it stink too. Has some kind of perfume on it. I had to make a mad dash from the closet. Drag almost caught me.

What is Loop going to do with this Jeff?

Said he needed an item that came in bodily contact with the victim in order for the cross to work.

Man, all this superstitious talk he's always carrying on, sometimes he gives me the willies with his talk. The other night he was playing poker and talking to himself and giving himself advice. He's always asking us to get things. Lucky you were able to lift that oil portrait from Drag's house. Loop sticks pins into it.

What is the meaning of it all Alcibiades?

Says he's practicing some religion that is so old that man left the caves with it. He said it's a magic. He says he's a sorcerer and that by making figures of his victims he entraps their spirits and is able to manipulate them—he said this is what early man did when hunting bison and elk. Don't say anything about it Jeff, we don't want to get my man uptight. We should be grateful to him for busting us out of jail in the last town where they were holding us on vag charges but I have to agree he's a little odd. Those expressions of his, Great Legba! and those chickens he's always sacrificing to crocodiles down at the marsh and the poems he's always writing.

He calls them curses.

The pair moved on past old Buicks and skeletons of washing machines, tramping over stone-aged ornaments and coins belonging to those drowned in underground rivers. Coins with terrible and grotesque scenes on them.

Alcibiades if we can hold on just a bit longer maybe we can fleece the cat of his money and make it on the Black Swan Stagecoach back to the East and write and paint some more. They don't care how sensitive you are out here in the old West.

I agree Jeff, this town Yellow Back Radio is weird and that Loop seems to have some gripe against society—see how he wasted the poor ranchers in the last town, kidnapped their wives' minds and strung out the kids, made some kind of cave into an underground discothèque called The Fiberglass Bat. He said that was just a mock-up of what's going to happen here. He is sho silly. Don't even comb his hair. Looks like buckwheat or alfalfa. Kee kee.

The men finally reached an opening in the cave. In the center of this area was a natural fire. Loop Garoo was dressed in a white smock. He wore glasses black skin-tight gloves and held a knife in his hand. On the floor lay a dead cock. Behind Loop stood an altar covered with cloth. It bore photographs of victims dead of strange whammies. Above this was a tapestry of a heart to each side of which were drawings of serpents.

Loop had just fed thirty pieces of silver to his personal Loa, Judas Iscariot, the hero who put the finger on the devil.

Did you get the item of clothing I requested? Loop asked of the men, removing his glasses and wiping them.

We did that brother Loop, Jeff said, handing him the scarf, whereupon Loop placed it near some cow tallow that had been made into candles. He started sprinkling some black powder on the scarf and repeating strange oaths.

Near some bottles set up on the altar was a small doll made of feathers, hair, snake skins and pieces of bone. It bore a resemblance to Drag.

The men sat in the corner, grinning, as Loop went through his motions.

The Loop Garoo Kid continued to sprinkle the black powder from his gloves.

This will give Drag Gibson the retroactive itch. It has fired his nerve endings already. This is just a test of what's to come. Testing . . . 1 . . . 2 . . . 3 . . . testing, Loop said, until the powder covered the entire neckerchief.

The men looked at one another, placing their hands over their mouths to suppress their humor.

O forgive me fellas, Loop said, there's some roast chicken, rice, green peas and turnip greens in bowls in the corner.

Thanks brother. We sure are hungry, Jeff said winking at Alcibiades.

In the corner of the cave, food and white wine lay on top of a red and black checkered table cloth.

This wangol will be so bad they will have to call in some of their top people, Loop murmured. It will be the strongest malice ever. Never again will they burn carnivals and murder children.

Loop Garoo began his tailor made micro-Hoo-Doo mass to end 2000 years of bad news in a Bagi he had built in the corner of the cave. He placed offerings to his Loa near jugs resting on several altars under a laced canopy embroidered with such emblems as skulls, crossbones, swords, serpents and hearts. The Loa's food, sea shells, playing cards, cigars, rum, thirty pieces of silver and oddest of all a pair of Everlast boxing gloves were neatly placed on the calabashes.

Taking a pinch of maize flour from a plate Loop began to draw on the floor in front of the altars various symbols associated with the Loa he wanted to call.

Loop began to shake a rattle slowly.

I the Father which wert in heaven conjure and command thee
O Legba master of the crossroads to connect this cowboy's
*   circuit to Guinea and summon forth:*

Cousin Zaka who will parch their fields and slaughter their
*   livestock and make their herd winding up the Chisholm*
*   stumble into a Twilight Zone*
O Gu rust their firearms and cause their horseshoes to slip
*   off the animals' hooves*
O Judas Iscariot who ratted on the Ghoul give me the
*   treachery to turn this town upside down and spill evil*
*   from all of its pockets*
O Jack Johnson give me the power to rise for the bell until
*   Yellow Back Radio is down for the count*
O Doc John, Doc Yah Yah and Zozo Labrique Marie Laveau
*   the Grand Improvisers if I am not performing these rites*
*   correctly send the Loa anyway and allow my imagination*
*   to fill the gaps*

O Mack Hopson blood of my blood teach me the secret of
    the 12 rabbits and the cheesecake
O Baron-La-Croix grip Drag Gibson so that every other day
    last rites will be requested
O Johnny of the delicate feet
Red-Eyed Ezili
Marinette of the dry arm send the dead swiftly to make my
    vengeance so complete and artsy craftsy that I though
    an amateur will be admired by houngans the world over
O General Dig, bury Drag Gibson in the stomach of wines
    next to George Wallace
O Black Hawk American Indian houngan of Hoo-Doo please
    do open up some of these prissy orthodox minds so that
    they will no longer call Black People's American
    experience "corrupt" "perverse" and "decadent." Please
    show them that Booker T and the MG's, Etta James,
    Johnny Ace and Bojangle tapdancing is just as beautiful
    as anything that happened anywhere else in the world.
    Teach them that anywhere people go they have
    experience and that all experience is art.

The leaves outside of the cave began to stir as in the
black of night demons started to camp about the land.

The ceremony completed Loop led a Billy Goat from a
heap of straw where the animal had been placed to
the very center of the area.

After slaughtering the animal Loop drank some of its
blood from a wooden bowl.

This will indeed be the super-hero hype to end them all,
Loop thought.

The men Jeff and Alcibiades who had maintained silence
throughout the ceremony laughed aloud, no longer able

to muffle their mirth. Tears welled up in their eyes and they rolled about the cave holding their stomachs.

What's wrong men? Loop asked.

Nothing, Alcibiades said, it's just that we're programmed by the Hedda Hopper people from a wooden planet of wide black hats and stickpins. With gossip columnists invading our skulls you should not be surprised that we would ridicule anything we can't understand.

O I see, Loop said returning to the grave business at hand, that of putting the goofer dust from Drag's projected plot into a little bottle.

He removed some shiny black boots which hung near a colony of bats. On each boot was painted the emblem of a yellow chicken. He tried on a black fedora. Hanging above the altar was a whip made of bull's hide and python skin. It was tough and heavy and when it flew through the air it whistled.

In another section of the cave, green eyes began to purr. Loop looked at his watch. It was time to feed the black cats prowling about the cave.

The two men, finished with their meal, lay back and started to sleep off the food they had so eagerly panhandled. Loop worked on into the morning, mixing potions, chanting poems, making dolls and burning candles. Now all he needed was a horse.

● ○

The Germans attacked the next day. There had always been skirmishes to the north between these dauntless, hearty warriors and the cattlemen who taxed them heavily, rode off with their women, rustled their cattle, stole their best grazing areas and burned their corn.

A warrior blew a signal through the bone-horn from the top of Blackfoot Mountain.

The Marshal was standing in front of Big Lizzy's Rabid Black Cougar discussing his exploits against the Sioux when a battle ax grazed his right cheek and slammed throbbing with thin pieces of flesh into the wooden façade of the Saloon.

The next one cut him down and he staggered and fell into the mud below the horses' post.

The Germans burned down Yellow Back Radio in a matter of seconds—about the amount of time it takes for a station break. Their appetites for destruction whetted, they traveled to Drag Gibson's Purple Bar-B.

Skinny McCullough knelt in a pasture about three miles from the Big Black House. He was scouting for grazing areas for greenhorns who would make up next year's drive up the Chisholm. He was pleased because he had discovered grama grass, known to make happy contented cows. He held the blades of rich green feast in his hands and was about to ride back to the Big Black House to tell Drag Gibson of this choice discovery, when he saw something shining above a bush outside the fence. It was a helmet reflecting the sun's rays. On each side horns protruded.

There was a stir and the Chieftain and two warriors leaped over the fence yelling consonantal war whoops and whirling their maces.

Skinny had just enough time to mount his horse's sore back but even on foot the barefooted Germans were almost able to overtake him.

He found Drag asleep on the velvet couch, the historical romance, The Life and Times of Catherine the Great, *lying on the floor. Skinny waded through the empty bottles of Red-Eye and tapped the boss on his shoulder.*

Drag! Drag! Some kind of half-naked unsaddled infidel white men attacking nesters from the north blond-haired blue-eyed devils wearing bearskins!

Aw go on Skinny, you some kind of folk nut or something? Drag answered half asleep.

No boss, he said running to the laced green curtains. They're coming up the path right now.

Soon Drag lay on the floor, his head resting on the ankles of his dead foreman.

When the rest of the hands and the servants were scalped the warriors headed for the stable to steal the horses.

The barnyard was in an uproar with much cackling squealing barking braying neighing clucking meowing and even some strange new noises (the revenge of Horrible Hybrid!).

When they reached the entrance to the stable the Chief-tain stumbled backwards, his hands shielding his eyes.

Ugh! Vor crying oud loud! I hate green! Vill you get rid of mit der green. I tink I'm going to get kranky.

The warriors obediently walked over to the horse's stall and were about to chop off its head when it awoke—wringing wet and snorting from the affects of its recurrent nightmare.

A black villain with unusual attributes was standing over it. A white snake moved around Loop Garoo's neck, green with envy. It frowned above its pink eyes and whistled its pink tongue. From then on the Hoo-Doo cowboy would hagride the night holding the horn of the lone green horse.

III. She May Not Be The Rancher's Daughter
But She Sure Can Cook

Rocking on its axles, the Black Swan Stagecoach rumbled to the front of the Hotel the next evening. Mustache Sal held the hem of her dress and was helped down by a cowpoke the foreman had sent from the Purple Bar-B to fetch her.

I be from Drag Gibson's Purple Bar-B, ma'am. Are you Mustache Sal, da one who answered da ad: old ugly ignorant cattlerancher with lots of acres wants woman with unusual habits? ن

The woman nodded at the fool and smiled as the man helped her into the buckboard that was to take them to the ranch. The two occupants faced forward not noticing the horseman who could be seen riding behind them as soon as the moon appeared.

How long have you been working for the Purple Bar-B, driver? Mustache Sal asked Drag's hand, who sat next to her, whipping the horses.

Hogs gut

The man's senses reeled from the heavy perfume Sal wore imported from Gay Paree, "Hogcalls in Nocturne." Her busts were about to break out of the top of her velvet dress as he could well see when he turned to answer her.

Duh, I been here for two years, mahm, I likes it swell.

Mustache Sal removed a cigar from her purse and began to moisten it with her tongue darting through her round beckoning lips. What's his Dun & Bradstreet rating?

Duh, don't know no fellers go by that handle working up here. Miss Sal you sure you haven't gotten da Purple Bar-B mixed up with some other place? the driver said, an itchy feeling creeping about his groin.

What is your job here driver? Mustache Sal continued realizing that further probing of this hick would reveal him to be as simple as they come.

I'm da assistant to the wranglers. I pumps da spring water for da horses.

Mustache Sal removed her hat and lay her head in the driver's lap. Her silky black hair hung between his knees.

What's wrong Miss Sal you gettin sleepy? the driver asked straining to keep his eyes in front of him.

Can you pump good, driver man?

The driver felt the words become hot breath. Steam edged about his already inflamed lap.

Well I tries my best Miss Sal da hosses don't complain.

Mustache Sal unzipped his pants and rubbed the bulb of his organ about her gums.

The horses went crazy and ran about the edge of a cliff.

The driver pulled them to a halt.

Whoa there whoa you fillies.

He smacked Sal's hand.

Hey duh stop that you . . . you . . . female you I'm trying to keep my eyes in my teeth, I mean my nose has to be on da trail so that my ears won't break da harness I mean . . .

Mustache Sal had expertly pulled off the man's britches shoving him into the rear of the chuck wagon parked on the side of the road and soon that section of the vehicle began to yodel as if a hundred Memphis hillbilly bands had teamed up with a locomotive.

The moon smiled from crater to crater.

● ○

When they were inside the Big Black House of the ranch the cowpoke started bowlegged up the stairs. He reached the top, his hands weighed down with bags, his eyes downcast—too bad, because Drag appeared on the top landing. He scared the cowpoke so, he stumbled backwards. No wonder, because Drag was quite a sight. He wore a flat black hat with a string dividing his chin into two huge beery lumps, laced trousers, a red sash around his waist, tight-fitting shoes, and as he came down the stairs he began to snap some castanets together.

Mustache Sal raised her head and did a double take.

What have I gotten myself into this time? she thought.

A rose between his teeth, Drag continued down the stairs. When he reached the suitcase which had opened in the cowpoke's fall, he slipped and rolled down the steps like a huge barrel.

The servants who had been peeking from behind the curtains broke up. Drag rose to his feet, an aging buffalo patriarch with ragged stumps for legs, and fired into the curtain. Sounds of little feet could be heard running down the hall.

The cowpoke edged out of the room leaving it to Drag and his prospective bride.

Hi sweet stuff, you must be the mail order bride, here let me see your teeth. He held Mustache Sal by the jaw and she complied by opening her mouth. Good, he said sitting across from the woman. I'm a big man in these parts, fish fill my full I mean full fish my swim.

Yeah Mac, Sal said, I read your scrawl in the newspaper.

Good then you know that I'm really what counts, Drag said sitting on a tack and bouncing up his hands holding the seat of his pants.

What's in it for me? Sal asked. I mean, you know, what about my piece of the action?

Well there's a messy part to it, but we got separate bed-

rooms and I won't bother you. You don't have to worry
about me and women. I got my Bible and as much
Dharmas as the next fellow. Although I do hope you're
warmer when I bang you than the last one who wuz so
cold she give one frostbite of the penis as if your prick
was on an excursion in Antarctica go in like a normal
organ come out a seal haw haw . . . o igloo pussy—

O.K. O.K. I got yooz, Sal said.

It's a deal, he said crunching her fingers between his huge
hairy hands. I'll have the little chink show you to your
room.

The man came in picked up the baggage and started upstairs. Drag stroked his chin and gave the chinaboy a
dollar bill, and pondered the figure shaking its hips as it
went up to the second floor of the building.

Strange creatures, women, Drag thought. Well, wonder
what's for chow?

● o

Thunder stabbed the night. Long yellow daggers. It
rained on YBR—on the swinepit behind the gallows. Hogs
in trench coats. Downstairs of the Big Black House the
Dr. was playing poker with Drag Gibson on the eve of his
wedding.

Drag I've been thinking, you don't think the Loop Garoo
Kid could have anything to do with these strange events

—the black cow found with its neck broke this morning? Drag, those were peculiar people—those circus folk. Think they got some tricks up their sleeves, making plans out there beneath the sod where we buried them?

Naw Doc. Coon won't show his face in this town. We kilt off the injuns and we can take care of anything he has in mind, even if he managed to get across the desert.

Upstairs the door banged violently, the curtains flapped against the walls. Sal attired in a blue negligee, was combing her hair for bed.

I really got ahold of a john this time. Like those old guys in Club Harlem, Atlantic City, drop a dime of their lives just to sniff me. This guy looks like he's got a weak ticker—if I turn him out a couple of times he'll kick off and this will be mine. Maybe a little arsenic to ease it along.

She looked in the mirror and saw *him* and like the hungry balladeer she was she shrieked, Mitt man mitt man where you been so long O mitt man my beautiful darlin. The black-haired beauty's hand rushed to her jaw.

Loop Garoo moved towards her. Yeah bitch! I thought I told you to stay in the Attic.

Loop baby I just kept bumping into the fairy stone I do declare. A girl can't go on making one night stands all her life. I tried therapy but the Dr. turned out to be a Democrat. I even tried scientism Loop, gave up Las Vegas steaks, and even the swami tried to fuck me Loop —you know men, only one thing on their minds.

She walked over to the Kid, unbuttoned the diamond solitaires on his buckskin jacket and dug her long sharp fingernails into his chest. She mussed the hair underneath his shirt. The blue negligee became a heap around her ankles. She took his hand and pressed it against her naked buttocks which showed a scar here and there. Her right knee stood out between his legs. She was panting hard.

They caught me Loop. The old man, you know how he is, Loop, the other one just watched—as if the fishermen weren't bad enough he's really got a degenerate crew around him now. He does lewd dances and shows off his scars, he uses 12 types of make-up, and the old man he did things to me Loop, I bleed a little—but hold me Loop, don't be so cold, we can have swell times again like before, you know, sniff airplane glue, make a bee-line to the two reelers, take a spin in the flivver, like, do the things we used to do.

Loop hurled the woman to the floor where she dramatically rolled over.

Honey bunch what did you have to go and do that for?

You know why bitch. When she georgiaed me, you had to follow. She made a fool of me and now you and that other one with the fur trapper who's always handing me subpoenas. All of you made fools of me. I walked the streets and ate ugly soup. Only wallpaper of zigzag designs kept me company. And you wanted to go and party time. Even when she left I thought you might still be loyal—but when I called you that night for a sandwich you hung up the phone and I could hear you in the background, the glasses clinking, the laughter, and to add to the insult it was Christmas Eve.

He removed a long brand from the black bag he carried. He went to the fireplace and returned to where she lay on the floor, trembling and naked. Her feet were about ten inches apart and a forest lay between her thighs.

O Loop my mitt man. How I missed your good good loving. She closed her eyes and gritted her teeth as the poker pressed against her abdomen. Saliva formed around her lips, her tongue shot out over her lower lip and she yelled, no longer able to contain the pain and beauty of being branded with a Hell's bat.

LOOP GAROO GAROO! LOOP GAROO GAROO! LOOP GAROO GAROO!

What's going on upstairs Drag? the Doc asked.

The way things are going on around here it must be the barnyard crawling into the house, Drag answered.

● ○

At the wedding the next night Drag interrupted the festivities to make an announcement:

The likker was fine, folks, the fiddler really cooking and you've met my wife who I think is going to turn out fine, the last one being so cold she give one frostbite of the penis haw haw.

Skinny McCullough the foreman, red-eyed with tears chortled—too much boss, frostbite of the penis that's really rich.

Someone requested that Chief Showcase read some of his militant poetry. Everyone applauded as the savage made his way to the front of the dining hall.

The Wolf-tickets of Chief Showcase

eat out of me backwards paleface!
like, your mind is a prairie dog's hole;
your soul the wild cat's squall. like,
may you fill the yawn of boothill's sigh,
and coyotes trample the fence of your grave.
may goats dine on the black grass of your
plot and the evil one skin your genocidal
hides and sell it as old clothes to serpents
of the sea.

my people gave you roots and berries,
showed your trains the perilous cliffs;
taught you how to rope a steer and bled
themselves to salute you. monsters that
you were you knifed them in the back,
sent their children off to die;
made their squaws chew your boots,
paved over the forests with cold concrete.

eat out of me backwards paleface,
like, your mind is a prairie dog's hole;
your soul the wild cat's squall.

Hear that injun! Did you hear that injun! What bitter and tortured Americana. Hey Injun come over here and look up my dress, said one of the hurdy gurdy girls from the Rabid Black Cougar.

The injun was tipping over to this tall broad amid healthy applause when all at once a Japanese semanticist came out of the curtains.

I enjoyed your poems dear child of nature, but I must say your people have a tendency to overuse the word 'like.'

The injun was about to bring his imported tomahawk down upon the little man when a crash was heard at the garden door.

O I thought spade poets had gone up in tinder, said the town Preacher Rev. Boyd with his sideburns electrified. But before he got out of the house altogether he turned around. But I guess it's the puff of smoke that bewitches.

Because standing in the doorway in full regalia was none other than the LOOP GAROO KID.

Drag Gibson, wicked whiskey drinker, your Hoo-Doo Death will be a collector's item, your head will lie in excrement, the flies will feast upon it and their wings will drop off. The maggots will eat and turn blue. Only your own kind will savor you and even for them you will be their laxative.

Then the Loop turned on his heels and vaulted over the veranda wall.

Stunned Drag staggered back a few steps with his elbow shielding his eyes and with the other hand pointed to the aura in the door:

THE   LOOP   GAROO   KID   DONE   REACHED

VIDEO JUNCTION AND GOT HIS UNKNOWABLE
TOGETHER, SPECTACULAR ENTRANCE, CHARMS,
RIDING MY SYMBOL, FANCY BLACK BOOTS,
SILVER SPURS, BLACK BUCKSKINS WITH PINK
FRINGES, BLACK MAGICIAN TO END THEM ALL
PSYCHING UP A BALLOONED SPEECH OF GRAF-
FITI THAT WOULD ESTRANGE POPEYE—AFTER
EM BOYS, Drag hollered.

The cowpokes stood shaking in their boots—Chief Showcase was protecting the women, his arms outstretched
and a slight grin on his face.

Drag removed the scourge from his side and started to
whip the cowpokes about the arms and shoulders. I'll be
a Son of a Gun, you're not following my orders, I'll have
your tongues snipped. He continued to beat them about
the posteriors and the heads as they slowly filed out of the
House to pursue the Kid. (Actually they rode about
the Main House a couple of times pretending to follow
the boss's orders.)

Drag plopped to the floor bawling like a kid.

All of you women clear outta here you're bringing me
down.

Crying like mad, Drag mumbled to himself:

Twas only yesterday or so we burnt down the circus and
here he come today. O Lord why did I ever bring nigras
to the West—he done gone ahead and got some strange
magic he's whipping on me—even trying his hand at

heraldry. I got to get the old Woman in the Valley to match him trick for trick.

While all of this was happening the new Mrs. Gibson was looking on:

A few more strokes like this and the geezer will be a goner, then I'll inherit all the property, she said behind her hand to the audience. She went over to the man and knelt beside him.

Anything I can do for you Grandpops? she asked jaws packed with gum.

Yeah, get outta here! You smell bad! I want to be left alone. Boo hoo!

Suit yourself, the woman said, going upstairs to play with her cards.

Then Dr. came into the room from outside.

After what I've just seen I need a drink!

What did you see Doc? Can't be as bad as what happened here—

There was this cowboy—

Well the old Woman on the talk show—

See we was having the bridal party and—

And I never saw anything that even remotely resembled—

(silence)

Go ahead and tell your horror story Drag—

No after you Doc—

Well see the Old Woman on the talk show called me just
as I was on the way to your party and told me to come
over to the studio at the Hotel. I went over there Drag
and she was packing her earphones and scripts. All the
engineers were in the control room, transfixed. She said
that the Loop Garoo Kid come in there and put some bad
waves into her transmitter. She said the "demons of the
old religion are becoming the Gods of the new," cause
he put something on her that had her squawking like a
chicken. She said she heard they had openings in Tombstone, Arizona, a nice peaceful one-horse town. She said
she was thinking about going legit and pursuing a new
career.

Drag's mouth was wide open. HOW CAN HE BE IN
TWO PLACES AT ONE TIME? HE WAS IN HERE. I
SAW HIM HE INTERRUPTED THE WEDDIN PARTY.

And just as the two old friends were debating the latest
disaster, Skinny McCullough ran into the room:

Drag. Doc. The trail boss come in here on a horse. Before
he died he said the wranglers the eight cowboys and the
cook had been trampled trying to save the cattle who
were stampeded by Giant Sloths which is crazy Drag because not only have Giant Sloths been extinct in North

America but when they were browsing around the plains they were peaceful at that.

Drag fainted. The cowpoke who bore the message stood over Drag, scratching his head in bewilderment. Sobbing passionately the Doc cradled his old friend's head in his lap.

● ○

The next morning the cowpokes, on every other occasion men of muscle and verve, huddled together sheepishly in their bunk. Skinny was sitting in the middle of the room with his men gathered about him.

Don't look like things are going to improve around here a-tall. That Loop Garoo Kid coming on like seance smoke and the boss way overdue with hysteria. I'm not hankering to stay around here any longer. You hear that coyote last night—that shrill howl made beetles creep up and down my spine.

I agree with yooz Skinny, another cowpoke said. I'm going to take my roll and gallop on out of here. If he wants someone to herd them cattle he ought to see about importing Eskimos or something they would fit right into this weird irrational discontinuous landscape—cows herded by dogsled over sand, nobody'd know the difference, strung out as the townsfolk are.

Upstairs where the Doc urged him to rest after witnessing Yellow Back Radio's fall line-up of stars, Drag turned up

the volume of the closed circuit TV. A camera hidden in
the hay in the bunk swung around to where his hired
hands were deliberating.

Hey Chinee, Chinee, bring me a can of beer, this is getting
real interesting.

Yeah, Skinny continued. Marcia the hurdy gurdy girl I
brought up to the House for the wedding party last night
said I was loco for working up at this here place. It was
becoming the talk of the town what was going on up
here and that some of the citizens were having meetings
down in the city dump to decide whether to march up
here with torches and pour salt on this evil smell.

The other cowpokes began to shift their boots nervously
and cross themselves.

You see the Kid ride off last night? It was as if he were
lightning taking a hiatus from nature. Looked like two
ghosts were waiting for him. I could see only their outlines in the moonlight.

What you say we pick up our gear and make it, Skinny?

The other cowpokes needed no encouragement and began to get their stuff together.

Suddenly Drag's voice boomed through the intercom:

Men come on up here a minute. Something big is cooking on the range.

Shall we go Skinny and ignore that command?

Naw let's see what the victim wants. He's harmless enough, poor boss, on his last leg.

● ○

The cowpokes entered Drag's sick room.

Men sit down, the waning cattleman whispered. Things are taking an occult turn around this joint. I know it's been trying on you but just so happens that them fossils who climbed from the wall of some museum and wiped out my herd have left me about bankrupt. I need to send my remaining steer to market while it's still time. Thought you boys would be able to do that for me—but I feel some discontent in the ranks. What's your beef men? You can level with me.

Boss, might as well tell you . . . after last night we decided we don't want to go through no routine that Loop Garoo might be spinning from his hideout wherever that strange place might be. Why last night when we chased him after that apparitional episode he came up with at your wedding I'm telling you, boss, he rode off into the night like a comet and there were grim outlines of some other ghosts waiting for him on the hill. We just poor cowpokes Drag, we ain't no wizards or padres, so we decided to collect our money and move on . . . cut out of here.

That's too bad boys cause I just drew up a stiffycate that

would divide the land up so's you fellows would receive
a slice, sort of people's capitalism. Now we snuffed out
them obscene unwashed hooligans and I think we can
wipe out a whole battalion of zombies too. Whatya say
men?

You mean you're going to split up the take of your em-
pire with us?

That's what I had in mind Skinny. How else would I
repay you men for your loyalty?

The men went into a huddle to argue the pros and cons of
Drag's proposal. It didn't take too long—for the steerbusters were just as avaricious as Drag Gibson.

Well since you put it that way, boss, I guess we can stay
around to take another herd up the trail, Skinny finally
spoke up, communicating their decision.

The men shook Drag's hand and headed back to the
bunk. The revolt nipped in the bud, Drag turned on
the TV to witness the men trudging down the path on the
way back to their chores. The closed circuit TV and the
dictaphone stored in the kitchen were good ways to keep
tabs on his servants' activities.

He reached for the can of beer the chinaboy had brought
into the room. He drank some and spat it out.

Piss! Goddamn chinamen still up to their pranks. I'll take
care of them and them ungrateful cowpokes too as soon
as these monsters check out of my life.

Drag dozed off. Next to his bed was a clipping he'd cut
out of the newspaper.

> *want ads*
>
> *will do anything*
>
> *for coin.*   JWH

● ○

That evening the chinee interrupted Drag's snoring:

Two gentlemen to see you Meester Drag.

Two men walked into the room.

Well if it isn't my old friends Meriwether Lewis and
William Clark. Why we died and went to Hell together.
Come on rest your moccasins fellows. What brings you
out this way to Yellow Back Radio?

O we were skin tapping some injun drumbeats and we
heard you was sick so we thought we'd drop in and bring
you what the injuns call "milk of the great white father"
but to us is nothing but good old hooch.

Gee that's awfully swell of you Clark, Drag said to the
tall red haired man as he and his companion put some
whiskey kegs in the corner.

We're working for some loon, the President of the United
States, and he sent us out here to get some mammoth

bones and fish vertebrae. Crazy about fossils. Reads a lot and built a way-out mansion in Virginia. Always tinkering with mechanical devices and writes poetry on the side. A real weirdo, made Lewis his secretary and Lewis can't spell worth a lick, can you Lewis?

The buckskinned, bucktoothed, freckled faced man with two lines for eyes said Duh, naw Clark I can't spell worth a lick.

Nice set up you got here Drag.

O we're trying to get it together Clark. Takes a lot of work but I've done all right since I escaped from hell. Sometimes the decomposition smells and if you get real close you can get a whiff of formaldehyde but I use some heavy deodorants so I'm getting by. So you say you're working for some nut?

Yeah, collecting elk horns, the whole bit, but we ran into some Indians. The Mandans and the Arikara treated us real nice. Gave us dogmeat and their squaws to seduce. Man what living—those savages are so naive. We eat so much dog food we feel like barking sometimes, don't we Lewis?

Yeah Clark sometimes we're just arfing around through the Valley in heat for injun squaws.

The injuns were all skinned out here fellows. Only one left, Chief Showcase. I keep him on for gags.

But I'm not in a very joking mood today. Some cowboy —a nigger—is out here putting something on me that I don't know what the nigger's putting on me. Interrupted the wedding.

You got married, Drag?

Sure. Long black hair, olive complexion, firm tits, a real pretty penny.

Hey that sounds like the chick me and you balled on our way coming up the stairs! She asked me and Lewis to lend her three bills so's she could go to the apothecary and fill a prescription for arsenic. Lewis fucked her in the ass while she was blowing me then we put her through a double 69 and passed gas in her face while she stuck pins in the bottom of my feet—we gave her the money and took it out in trade. Sorry we stunk up your staircase Drag.

Yeah that sounds like her the way you size her up, fellows. How was it? I got her through the papers.

Man it was some good yelling, screaming pussy. She rolled her thighs and moaned so good me and Lewis come all over the rug on your stairs Drag. Sorry about that.

Well good, fellows, I'm glad she's warmer than the last one who was a very frigid number. I just married her cause I read in the *Psychiatric Journal* that evil can be passed on through the chromosomes so I decided to have some kids.

Gee Drag you're reading all the time. Why you read your way right out of Hell.

I don't know. I'm lost if this Loop keeps it up. I got aches all over from last night.

Maybe I can recommend something. I am a bit of an occultist pediatrician orthopedist, all that good stuff—maybe I can perk you up there some Drag.

Mighty nice of you Clark.

The explorer put a poultice and a string of wild onions around Drag's neck, and wrote down some other ingredients:

> salve of pine resin
> beeswax
> bear's oil
> and plenty of draughts of strong horse mint tea to drink.

Lewis stood in the corner enthralled with a yo-yo.

We'd better be pushing back to the East. Deal with some more of the injuns, Clark said. Most of them are cooperative but the Sioux were a little suspicious when we encountered them. Injun killing runs in the family. Why George Washington Rogers Clark cleaned out the Shawnee's settlements. Killed 10 chiefs, burned 500 Indian cabins and destroyed all the grain. Boy, my pa really loved to cut up. Maybe that *Psychiatric Journal* you was reading is correct there Drag.

Clark and Lewis were walking out of the room when something occurred to Clark.

Drag you said all the injuns were wiped out. Then what

were them drums we heard? Highly intricate rhythms mixed with what Frenchy Jefferson calls gutbucket.

Drag thought for a minute:

The idea of another tribe inhabiting these hills has about as much authenticity as a horse's dream. Wonder what it could be?

Confused, the explorers looked at one another.

Wiry spaced out sounds moved across the night outside.

● ○

Royal Flush Gooseman, aging unscrupulous fur trapper, adjusted his coonskin cap. He rode next to Mighty Dike, bulldyker octoroon. Her saran wrap cape stiffened, unyielding even to the wind. She wore goggles, bore a boyish haircut, and a leather mini-skirt with fur around the hem and jackboots. The bridge of her nose rested upon nostrils which seemed two chubby paws ready to spring. Behind was a long line of mules loaded down with calico firearms and very expensive beaver peltries with which Royal Flush expected to corner markets back East, beaver caps being very "in" that year.

Well, chocolate mama, we're in business now. We sold them defected flintlocks to the injuns, allowing the cattlemen to wipe them out. Wasn't it funny them crawling across the plains like that with their hands clasped to their necks? Glad we took pictures of it, I can sell them to the

Smithsonian. Won't be long, baby, before we're lying on the beach in Miami and your name up in lights. Aren't you glad you came away with me from that loser you were with?

You were absolutely right in, shall we say, selling the guy down the river, Royal Flush said, leaning over and nudging the woman in a wide belt she wore on her hips from which dangled chalky trophies from former lovers, penises which had been made into plaster of paris casts.

Now with the gold Drag gave us for them Coult rifles he used in blasting them kids who didn't believe in law and order, to use a popular euphemism, I'll be able to sub-lease Florida.

O Royal Flush you thrill me so, she said riding the mule and examining her fingers glittering against the snow. All the things you've done for me, Cadillac, buckboard and cooperative mules, all a girl could desire, Fire Island in the summer!

O yes Royal I'm all yours, she said leaning over and bussing the furtrapper on the cheek. He was nothing but a jeffing con. When Diane went uptown, me and Sal hat up too. I think she's still in love with him, that Sal, maybe Diane too but I'll fix the nigger. I'll have him subpoenaed and thrown in jail if I see him again. The way he used to brand me and beat me leaving those welts in the shape of bats on my fine yellow frame.

Down below is the town of Yellow Back Radio, Drag's town, Gooseman pointed out. He said we can stay there for free in his Hotel. As long as we want. Some old dame gives out the weather reports and runs down the produce scores. Sometimes she indulges in astrological predictions.

The two rode down Blackfoot Mountain until they came into view of the buildings lined up. Behind the Executioneer's display, hogs with armored jaws were chewing on some metal scraps. Before they came to the road that connected with Main Street, Royal Flush looked over his shoulder and took inventory of his stock: furs, quackbottles, saddles, carbines, kitchen knives, calico dresses, sun bonnets, snuff, tobaccy, photographic equipment. He flapped his stirrups against the mule's side and spat out a long cigar, and rubbed his hands. O.K. doll, let's go get these palookas.

O Royal Flush you're so cute, Mighty Dike cooed, pecking the merchant on his shiny head.

● ○

The saddle stiffs from the Purple Bar-B were congregated in Big Lizzy's Rabid Black Cougar drinking Rot-Gut and Two-Bits-Per-Throw. Some of the cowpokes were seated at tables playing poker or being entertained by the hurdy gurdy girls.

Skinny McCullough the foreman was at the bar conversing with Sam the bartender.

Man, that boss is really getting timid in the noggin, Skinny said.

Can you blame him? Monstrous births, weird parties, his nag stolen, herd wiped out by mysterious animals, toes, fingers and hindlegs rotting away, I mean how can you blame the guy? But I don't care if he turns into black straw so long as he coughs up the deeds he promised us.

He brings us up there every Sun, and he reads those awful words from the good book. Sometimes I feel so skerry I go back to my bunk and have dreams in which blank-eyed and stupid demons do handsprings on my chest. I think as soon as this season comes to an end I'm going to take my roll and go over to join the Lincoln County forces against that anarchist bandit Billy the Kid. It's nice and peaceful on the front.

Did you see his latest symptoms? the bartender said. Sits up there on the hill. Got all the servants building a monument he designed for himself. Said he might kick off any day now. Case he feels it coming and wants to get it over with quick. And to add to that each night the coyote howls outside his house and he raises himself and sez: Who's that! Who's that howling about my door?

Good evening Marshal.

Good evening Sam, Skinny. Damn, what time of day is it? Looks half and half, like a land assessor's coffee break. Let's have something special today. Hows about some of that imported Lacrymose Christi?

Marshal, Skinny said, I was just telling the bartender that Drag is getting spookier than a son of a bitch. He's a mere whisper of his former self. Each morning we find those effigies on the doorstep. Before you know it he'll be making

an appearance before the Riders of Judgment. He thinks
the Loop Garoo Kid has put some kind of so-called
magical spell on him or something. While he's out there
building his tomb that new mail order bride of his plays
with them funny cards.

Poker?

No, some kind of weird cards, one of em had death on it,
with a scythe cutting across the grim reaper's foot.

You don't believe in that malarkey do you boys? the Marshal asked.

No I'm a Fanny Wrightite, Skinny said.

And I'm a Baptist, the bartender offered, that pagan nonsense cuts nothing with me.

Just then Royal Flush Gooseman, Furtrapper and sometimes bald-headed Cowthief, and Mighty Dike entered
the room:

O.K. all you brush poppers, ranahans, limb skinners, and
saddle warmers, this is Royal Flush Gooseman all the
way from St. Louis!!!!!!!!

All the cowpokes rose from their tables with gosh, golly
stares on their faces. The Marshal and bartender and the
foreman were a little more nonchalant, each having been
as far as the Mississippi River a few times apiece.

What you need, cowpokes? Rectifyers to heal them
bruises, blankets, boots, firearms, bottle of rum all the way

from Boston? Come outside and inspect my mule train. You got the money I got the time.

Little hand of poker while you're at it. I even got posters of that greenhorn President of the East case you want to mount them on your bunk walls and spit tobaccy at em.

All the buckaroos laughed and followed Royal Flush outside to examine his mule train of goods. Some of them were already reaching into their jeans for silver with which to make purchases.

The Marshal, foreman and bartender continued their conversation.

Man, pass me another whiskey. This place is really getting eerie, never seed no town like this; all the planks holding up the buildings seem to lean, like tilt over, and there's a disproportionate amount of shadows in reference to the sun we get—it's like a pen and ink drawing by Edward Munch or one of them Expressionist fellows.

Huh?

See, got me talking out of my noodle. What's your theory Marshal? Skinny McCullough asked.

Well you know me, boys, why if I hadda been at that party the other night instead of at the Law Enforcement Convention up the creek there, it would have been me and the Kid. Hell, me and the Earp brothers use to ambush people and shoot em in the back like they wuz dogs. He'd better not show his snake in Yellow Back Radio.

Big Lizzy the owner of the Rabid Black Cougar entered. A giant square-jawed woman with a tomboy haircut, her flabby breasts hung around her roped in waist. She wore an apron over a drab calico dress, with leggings and boots, and her hands were covered with hair. Below the nose bridge could be seen the faint print of a mustache.

She spoke in a low husky voice that sounded like sand paper rubbing together. She carried a moose over her shoulder and under her arm a Winchester Rifle.

Evening Big Lizzy, what's that you got with you? Well I'll be, the Marshal said scratching his head, it's a moose!

Yeah, Lizzy answered, bagged him up in the hills while I wuz hunting. She swung the moose over her shoulder and onto the floor. Chinaboy go get me some beer mugs out of the latrine so's I can give the boys a drink and clean up that ear that wuz shot off a couple of weeks back, it's beginning to smell. I need a drink of Red-Eye after what I saw up there in the hills.

Whaddya see Big Lizzy? Skinny asked.

There was this woman cooking some smelly stuff in a cauldron. I came upon her about the third evening out. She was stirring with some long pole, when all of a sudden this black cowboy come riding out of the shadow and hitched up her skirts and whipped his pecker on her right on the spot. I had to put my hand on the dying moose's mouth so he wouldn't make no noise, cause then things really started to freak out.

What happened then Big Lizzy? one of the steerbusters

gambling at the table asked as the others put down their cards and gathered around the bar to listen closely to Big Lizzy's strange narrative.

Well they were on the ground making out and she started to writhe and hiss like a serpent and say skerry things like: mash potatoes all over my motherfucking soul. Then after it was over he gathered her up and they rode off to the cemetery where tombs shone against the moon like white plates.

How did the woman look? Skinny asked.

She was wearing shades even in the night, a black velvet dress and a jade locket. Had long black hair and olive skin. A real beauty. Bilt like a brick shit house.

Hey that sounds like the boss's old lady, one of the hands said. Let me go up to the ranch and tell him he'd better see about his old lady.

The foreman grabbed the man by the collar:

Hold on you idiot, wait until the season's over. The way he's wasting away like he might be in a vile mood. You see how he flogged us the other night, next thing you know he'll be asking us to milk the cows or something harebrained like that. Be cool till the eagle flies, that way we won't get in Dutch.

The cowpokes who had gone outside with Royal Flush returned loaded down with goods. One went to the group at the bar.

Geez you know he cleaned us out. Had a little stand set up in the street and had Royal Flushes in poker four times straight, never seed nothing like it!

The Marshal, foreman, Big Lizzy and the bartender chuckled.

What happened to the last wife? Big Lizzy inquired.

She's up in the hills Big Lizzy, tomato, in the plural these days.

O I see.

Big Lizzy ever since we burnt down the circus strange things have been happening. There was this nigger bull-dogger guy who performed. He could bring down steer with his teeth and he used a whip like most men fire a pistol. Anyway he rode off and the townspeople haven't come down from those devil's pills them wicked kids gave them, them horrible urchins we knocked off.

Town 50 miles from here the kids were found in caves smoking injun tobaccy and the herd Drag sent up the Chizzum was stampeded by Giant Sloths which is crazy as hell Big Lizzy, cause Giant Sloths haven't lazed around the Plains of North America for thousands of years. Sometimes I think the whole continent is accursed.

The Preacher Rev. Boyd is going around like the town kook. Nobody goes to his Church any more and he's weaving some kind of allegorical prophecies.

The Preacher Rev. Boyd entered the bar and through his

three week old beard began to recite from a yellow pad attached to a clipboard. He reeled about the room.

stomp me o lord!!
i am the theoretical mother of all insects!!
mash my 21 or so body segments!!
tear the sutures which join my many abdomens!!
make me a mass of stains of thy choice
an ugly blotch under thy big funny clodhoppers!!

The door swung open on the last line.

The men seated dropped their poker cards and slowly moved away from their chairs. The moose got to its feet and clomped through the side of the building, sending splinters of wood flying.

Hear you're looking for me, Marshal.

Big Lizzy, Skinny McCullough and the bartender eased away from the bar. The other cowpokes froze.

Now Kid, the Marshal said, what's a Western without tall tales and gaudy romance? Have a drink.

Pretending to reach for his change the Marshal drew his shooting iron. Too bad. Too slow. Not fast enough. ☺

The lash whistled across the room and popped off the Marshal's holster, a second lash flicked the gun from his hand, a third lash cracked off the Marshal's hat, a fourth lash unbuckled his belt with its persuader, which caused the Marshal's pants to fall, and came within a thousandth

of an inch of his shirt, unpinning the star, which dropped
to the floor.

The moose peeked in through the big hole he had made
in the wall, but seeing no improvement in the situation,
galloped towards a lake in the distance.

Loop Garoo the lord of the lash walked over to the end of
the bar to where the Preacher was crouched on the
floor.

He was scribbling furiously on his yellow pad.

When he saw the Loop standing over him, Rev. Boyd
brought forth his crucifix. Nothing happened. He took out
a pocket mirror and aimed it into Loop's face. Loop used
the opportunity to straighten his fedora which had slid
to the side of his head when he gave the Marshal such a
good behind whipping.

Finished? Loop asked.

The Preacher backed away a few paces with a dipshit grin
on his face.

Loop lashed the crucifix from his breast without tearing
into the man's flesh. The crucifix dropped to the floor and
the little figure attached to it scrambled into the nearest
moose hole.

Didn't you say something about spade poets having gone
up in tinder when I walked into the party the other night?
Come on Preacher don't start your thing, I don't want to
hear anything about Matthew Chapter and Verse in ditty

bop talk. I get sick of "Soul" sometimes. All right then, Loop said.

(CRACK!) Whenever you say something like that. (CRACK!! CRACK!!) In the future. Check out some sources. (CRACK!! CRACK!!) Motherfucker!! (CRACK! CRACK!) Ask you mama. (CRACK!) Yo wife. (CRACK! CRACK!) Guillaume Apollinaire. (CRACK! POP! CRINKLE! SNAP!) Anybody you want to ask. (CRACK!) But get your information right next time. (NICK!) O.K.?

The Preacher lay on the floor a quivering mumbling heap.

Loop folded his whip and looked about the room. He winked at Big Lizzy. Anybody else want some of this ringing stinging?

The cowpokes shook their heads.

Loop put a rolled cigarette into the Marshal's mouth and walked outside the bar. The townspeople who had been peeking through the door ran in different directions.

Loop mounted his green horse which kind of did a slow high-stepping trot out of town.

The Marshal just stood there for a moment taking a long swig of whiskey. Big Lizzy's eyes were two lights she was so much in glee. Her jaws swelled with laughter. The cowpokes all stood, pushing their feet around the floor and eyes downcast in embarrassment.

The Marshal picked at the edges of his mustache. His eyes became moist. He knelt and picked up his badge. He

pulled up his pants, covering his red and black colored
BVD's.

Well folks, I'm not going to make excuses. The Kid made
a fool of me. Got nothing on but my shorts. I'm a scoun-
drel, a rogue and a bully. Later for Yellow Back Radio. I've
met my match here so now it's time to move on down
the line.

He shook hands with everybody in the bar then walked
outside and stood in front of the saloon.

The street was a dumpheap of Brueghel faces, of Ho-
garth faces, of Coney Island hot-dog kissers, ugly pusses
and sinking mugs, whole precincts of flat peepers and silly
lookers. The sun's wise broad lips smiled making the goats
horny with cosmic seed as monstrous shapes who could
never unbend their hands all looked as the Marshal
ripped off his badge, boarded his horse and rode out of
town. Each side was lined with spectators. He rode past
his beloved Hat and Boot store, the Feed store and on
into the Black Forest.

IV. If It Had Been A Snake It Would Have Bit Him

Chief Showcase sat on the porch of the Big Black House puffing on his water pipe and nodding. He was getting some cool. The sky was packed full of stars and once and a while one would speed across the heavens.

It was in the quiet of the night and one lone light could be seen in the bunk house where some of the cowpokes had stayed up to play a hand of cards. From far away came the low howl of a coyote.

Mustache Sal walked out on the porch. Her black hair, alluring and glossy, hung down to her waist. She leaned against the post and stared at the stars.

Do you know those visitors who were here to see Drag, Chief Showcase?

Chief Showcase's eyes slowly opened.

You talking to me, Mrs. Gibson?

Yes Showcase, those men who were here, what did they want?

O it's some of those men who were your husband's Vice Presidents of the great Atrocity Corporation that tumbled into Hell after the last crash.

O I see Chief, thanks for the info. What are you doing out here this time of night? I thought Indians were afraid of the dark.

We're not as afraid of the dark as some of these strong he men type cowboys around here. Some of these fighting quarrelsome demons sitting on the top of the Big Black House that have been appearing have really gotten the help shook loose.

O you don't believe in all of that, do you Chief Showcase? I mean a handsome redman like yourself could never be taken in by a loony nigger. My husband will have his scalp in no time. Besides the lease to the underworld is in my name. I tricked him into signing it with my wily charms.

Let's just say that I'm not taken in as much as the Loop Garoo Kid was taken in by you.

What did you say Chief? Mustache Sal said, walking with her hands on her hips towards where the Indian sat.

Nothing Mrs. Gibson.

Mustache Sal slid down next to Chief Showcase. Call me Sal, Injun, she said her huge bright eyes shining behind her shades. What is that you're smoking?

The Chief handed his employer's wife the water pipe. Mustache Sal's brain began to tingle.

Whew, what kind of tobaccy is this? Mustache Sal said closing her eyes.

Tobaccy hell! Bought a mule caravan full of the stuff when I flew over to Nepal last year.

You travels a lot Redskin.

Sure do.

Next time Drag calls you up to the Big House for one of those conferences he's always having with you maybe you can drop in and tell me about your travels.

Drop in like what you did to Drag's cups with those little pills?

Who told you about that?

Just a half hour before you came downstairs you dropped them in his cups. I saw you on Drag's closed circuit TV I routed through to that little teepee servant's quarters they built for me down near the outhouse.

You won't tell will you? Mustache Sal pleaded, rubbing against Chief Showcase and starting to unbutton her blouse.

What does white folks business have to do with me, Showcase said lifting her long black skirts and placing his hand upon her creamy thighs. The white man has the brain of Aristotle, the body of Michelangelo's David and the shining spirit of the Prime-mover, how would it look for a lowly savage and wretch such as me meddling in his noble affairs? Showcase said piledriving into Sal so that her spine rammed up against the wall of the porch banner and her legs wrapped about Showcase's hips.

O pump me until your marvelous dick turns to gold . . .

Showcase put his hand over the boss's wife's mouth. Be quiet and deal, Showcase said rolling from side to side and pushing deeper.

● ○

Mustache Sal lay in her bed silly and mumbling in euphoria from the all night love-making she'd received in Chief Showcase's arms. The heathen had told her to deal and deal she did until the good good loving had spread throughout her body so that her blood throbbed at his touch. When he came he shouted war whoops. That was something. They had screwed over and over again until exhausted and spent they could get at it no more. Showcase had dragged himself to his little Teepee and she had somehow managed to get upstairs.

She glanced at the clock on the dresser which stood in front of her grand four poster with brass rails. Funny that they had coupled on the porch and no one could hear them. That made it even more exciting balling while at any moment some cowpoke would stumble upon them.

It was seven o'clock, time to get up. The birds were chirping and she could hear the chinaboys downstairs preparing pancakes. Her thoughts returned to Chief Showcase. Where did he learn that little trick he pulled on her after the fifth orgasm? He had called it the little man in the canoe. Something else, this Indian. For the first time she understood where Tonto was at. And the reason for the

white man's mask or as high-falutin' folks say, persona.
They ought to change his name to Chief Feelgood.

That's it, Chief Feelgood the Hawk in a Woman's Valley.
She'd have to ask Spooky Situation to do it—since Showcase was his ward there'd be no problem.

Spooky Situation—the arsenic!

She put a robe around her nakedness clutching the collar
around her neck so as to conceal the impressions made by
the redskin's teeth. She ran into her husband's room.

Sure enough Drag had kicked the bucket and the milk
was drying in the dirt. Green all over. Mustache Sal
pulled the sheet over his head and ran downstairs to the
kitchen where the chinee servants were preparing break-
fast.

Ring the bell for the cowpokes. My husband is dead!

Mustache Sal ran upstairs to put on some clothes. Confetti dropped from the kitchen windows while the servants did a little jig and popped balloons. They rang the
come-and-get-her-while-she's-juicy-and-hot bell.

Once inside the cowpokes sat down at the table. Mustache Sal was all in black and had her face screwed up in
a widow's pose. A high collar covered her previous night's
passion.

Gentlemen I'm afraid my husband's dead. From now on
I'll pretty much run things around here—so all of you who
work on the Purple Bar-B will have to answer to me. I'm

sorry to have to bring you such negative news so early in the morning.

That's all right Missy, the chinaboy said his legs crossed and his eyes closed in merriment.

Suddenly Spook-Off appeared at the top of the steps snatched in the nick of time from the jaws of death, as it were.

Negative, I got your negative, Drag said holding up some undeveloped snapshots.

You put arsenic in my milk you fucking cow. It's all on tape. You and that nigger out in the woods doing the mambo some kind of new licentious filthy dance and hollering Chief Showcase's name so loud last night I couldn't sleep and even dropping your funky drawers to my visitors.

Don't get me wrong, I didn't mind all of you guys getting laid but she is so cruel that she wouldn't even allow me to come and look through the keyhole. I played dead and put some green paint on my face so's I'd catch you in the act.

Grab hold of her boys.

The two cowpunches grabbed her arms. She tried to twist from their grasp.

I'm not licked yet, Drag said.

Yeah we knew she'd been running around on you boss, that's the spirit.

Put her in the swine pit.

Upon hearing this instruction, as cold-blooded a varmit as Skinny McCullough was, the rolled cigarette fell from his lips and he stepped back a few paces along with the other hands.

Boss don't make us do that, Skinny said. As mean as I am I wouldn't want that to happen to a dog. Those carnivorous and horrible critters whom even self-respecting hogs avoid. Trained by that alienated and Faustian hangman, they only prey on humans in that little yard of theirs behind the scaffold. Please boss don't make us do it.

YOU OLD FAT AND UGLY BASTARD IF YOU DO THAT TO ME MAY FAGGOTS MAKE YOU TRIP INTO HELL, Mustache Sal screamed.

Ho hum, Drag thought, these prophecies was all over the joint these days. Seemed like every tramp off the street was trying to start some new fangled religion.

Take her away.

Some of the men reluctantly dragged the screaming woman out of the House and threw her into the buckboard for the trip to the swine pit behind the gallows.

Rest of you guys come upstairs, Drag said inviting the rest of the cowpokes to his library for a confab. The shelves were full of yellow kivered books and volumes on

the life of the benevolent despotess Catherine the Great
whose manner of death made her heroine of cowboys all
over the world.

The calf thumpers reverently took their hats off and
walked with great care upon the plush rugs that covered
the stairs leading to the second floor.

Once inside the library Drag addressed them: Men,
as you know things have become outta sight around here.
This black-as-the-ace-of-spades-monster-with-midnight-
for-Shiva-arms is giving us such heebie jeebies that it's not
safe to water the cows, mine the minerals, and take care
of business in the barnyard.

Amen, said the cowpokes nodding their heads in agree-
ment.

But I want to tell you that we got a plan to get rid of
this spook once and for all. Because in the other room
there is the greatest ghost chaser of all the West. Some
one of whom it was said, "that boy can handle a pistol
fastern a frog can lick flies."

I give you, Drag said, rising to his feet, the baddest coon
skinner of them all—killed many people. Many of them
the meanest and baddest woogies. John Wesley Hardin.

The men stood but nothing happened.

I SAID COME IN JOHN WESLEY HARDIN.

A tall man with a heavy mustache and blue eyes walked

into the room to a full round of applause from the cowpokes, some of whom jumped up and down.

Sorry I missed your cue there Drag but I was looking at
your copy of the good book. You know St. John on how
filthy and awful womens is. Reminds me of the time they
put me in jail in Huntsville, Alabama and made me the
Sunday school superintendent. I got so strung out behind
the Bible that I went on to study Law. Got my degree in
jail. I've always been on the side of the Word, killing only
those who were the devil incarnate—you know—black
fellows.

But anyway Drag, to get to the business at hand, I understand you got some wild and woolly crow over here that's
about to worry you to death.

You said it Johnny boy, why I think I'll be roping the last
Steer if he keeps it up.

John Wesley Hardin felt the cap-ball .44 Coult stuffed
under his shirt.

Nothing to fear, John Wesley Hardin is here Drag. My
contempt for niggers is very well known. When I was 15
which is about 60 years from now I killed some insolent
devil who didn't know his place. It was after the Civil War
and the nigger was feeling good. Well they sent some
Yankees and I blasted them over too. Next I found 5 of
them coons swimming in a pond and shot them out of
the water. I fired so fast the lake bounced up and down
and the fish had to go to some kind of neptune analyst
the next day, they couldn't believe it.

That's all right, that is really choice, the cowpokes mumbled.

By the time I was 17 I had wiped out 7 men. Decided to settle down, I married to raise stock. But by then it was too late. Broke out in sweats in the middle of the night. It had become an obsession. I went out and found me a black policeman and had him on the ground wriggling and convulsing from the lead I pumped into him.

They put me into jail, them Yankees. But I sawed out of a jail in Texas and went and found me some more happenings and lynched a Negro because by this time that was more kicks than eating, fucking, or getting stoned.

Just then a white python fell from the chandelier and coiled itself around John Wesley Hardin, its ruby red tongue and eyes staring directly into the famous gunslinger's face.

John Wesley Hardin began to wiggle and stagger around the room as Drag and the cowpokes looked on helplessly.

Certain psychologists have said that human beings have a way of blocking experiences too awful for the senses to accommodate. So it was in the old West.

John Wesley Hardin and the snake were now against the wall of the room sliding down to the floor.

an aside?

An unusual calling card don't you think? Standing in the door was the Loop Garoo Kid.

I told you, Drag Gibson, that no amount of romantic dosage is going to save your neck, dead man. Heroes given to hyperbole—I even chased the Marshal out of town! Besides, when you want me, come and get me yourself.

The cowpokes were pretending to be in a dentist's office of the mind. They had their heads buried in magazines.

Loop went over to the corner and removed the python from the prostrate man's body. John Wesley Hardin's hair had turned completely white. His pupils were crosses.

Dressed in his black shirt and pink fringed black buckskin, Loop coolly walked out of the room and down the stairs to the green horse waiting outside in the shadows.

The men sat in silence and stared at their last hope, out cold and mad looking in the corner.

Drag had fallen from the chair. It looked as if the cattleman was about to give up the ghost. The cowpokes cried. Outside the night cried pouring down hard on the crying barnyard. The fruit on the trees was covered with icy fluid and the whole valley seemed to throw up its hands in despair.

● ○

Loop Garoo, the python tucked away in his saddle bags, rode through the town of Yellow Back Radio towards

the swine pit trough behind the gallows. He removed
his black fedora and paused for a minute of silence.

He tossed a red rose into the pit where hogs were chewing
on their dessert—a black velvet dress covered with blood.

That's the breaks, Loop thought riding back to the cave
to get on with the serious business of closing every con-
ceivable repair shop available to Yellow Back Radio, whose
signals were needless to say becoming very very faint.
In fact it seemed that the whole valley would soon be off
the air.

● ○

Field Marshal Theda Doompussy Blackwell sat on a
white crate in his office. The doorman's coat covered his
long johns to about two inches below his knees. A wig
lay lopsided on his shivering head and his dentures were
on the floor next to a bucket of hot water in which his
feet rested.

He was sobbing and listening to a recording of "Yankee
Doodle Dandy" which came from a Victrola horn in the
corner of the room. Besides the white crate it was almost the only other furnishing. Not quite. On a wall was
the famous petrified moose head.

Pete the Peek, Congressman, professional voyeur and
Theda's co-conspirator groucho marxed into the room,
picked up Theda's dentures and pushed them into the
black hollow of the soldier's mouth. He then fixed the

wig which was about to fall from the Field Marshal's head, and with a white monogrammed handkerchief dabbed at the tears rolling down his cheeks.

Thanks honey I'm so cold I'd freeze if I picked them up myself.

Think nothing of it, the Congressman said squatting in the corner.

They both swung their heads in time to the music until the needle got stuck on macaroni macaroni macaroni macaroni . . .

Pete lifted the arm from the record and returned to his place in the corner. It was close to 12 A.M.

I just had enough time to take off my pajamas when I got your message Theda. Geez I was having dis nightmare about some Hoo-Doo nigger cowboy who took over a radio station and broadcast strange fixes, laying a trick on a Western town. I forget da name. Anyway it got so bad dey had to call in da Pope to straighten tings out. Da bad dream ended with pigs with scrap iron for teeth doing da re-cap. It really got into me. My lips were wet and was screaming, "Mama Mama Mom O Mom help your baby." It was a deep trip Theda; it was as if I had to don a snorkel and rubber suit to go through da black pools of my shut-eye. I woke up on da floor in a heap of panties, bras, lipstick tubes strewed about my bedroom. See me and da guys had a caucus last night. After it was over I wuz stuck with dis real dog who remained when all da other guys got good lookin pancakes and left. I wuz about to stick da pig when I dozed off and dat's when I had da dream. I had to go into da kitchen and have da maid prepare me a late snack out of da frig— Kentucky Bourbon chased with water.

Well what about me? Field Marshal Doompussy Blackwell said squirming on his white crate. Does this look like my outfit to you? And why do you think my wig is all nappy and only a few patches of powder cover my decrepit yellow face? I didn't even have time to place a mole on my cheek I rushed over in my carriage so fast. The doorman was doll enough to lend me his coat.

What's up, Theda, is Frenchy up to his old tricks again? Pete asked dipping into a snuff box and removing the funnel from his head.

You said it Peter. O they treat me so mean—do you know what that child did this time?

No Theda, what?

Appropriated 2500 dollars so's a couple of ruffians could go hunt mammoth's bones and various botanical specimens to add to his Americana collection at Monticello. Can you get to that? Here I am in charge of Defense and I have to go around in ragged sneakers and borrow the doorman's coat because to tell you the truth honey I was ashamed to wear my General's outfit. I don't even have enough money to take it to the cleaners. He said he didn't believe in standing armies and that a good revolution from time to time is good.

Did he say dat Theda?

Said it as sure as you're standing before my eyes. Why that's why he got his ass out of Virginia that time when the British invaded and he was Governor. Said he was too busy inventing a cyptographic device called a wheel cypher to be concerned with force of arms.

Yeah Theda, remember dat time he was almost busted when he was ambassador to France and he was recuperating from an ailment in Italy and was seen smuggling Po Valley rice so's he could compare it to da rice grown in Carolina?

Gossip has it that he spent most of his time learning the process by which parmesan cheese was made and learning how to make macaroni. And you know what else, Pete?

No, the Congressman answered, as Theda leaned over and whispered into his ear.

Likes niggers a whole lot.

You don't mean it.

I kid thee not. When he was Gov of Virginia he tried to have a law passed against slavery and then later on wanted to banish slavery in the territories.

And he spends a lot of his time womanizing.

And remember what he did to the old man John Quincy Adams, Pete? I won't forgive him for that as long as I live. This impudent obscene underground pamphleteer accused the old man of giving all the baboons the original

red ass and when the old man retaliated against all of
those liberals, anarchists, beatniks and what have you by
getting through the Alien and Sedition Acts, high and
mighty couldn't even be a loyal Vice President—he
pushed through his Kentucky resolution which declared
the President's act illegal. Took it upon himself.

Well whaddya expect, Theda, look at all of dem far-out
amendments he got pushed through da Constitution. He
looks down his nose at us Congressmen, I see him, just
because he can do fol de rol, calculate an eclipse, tie an
artery, plan an edifice, break a horse, do a mean minuet
and play da fiddle, he ain't so smart, why look.

O Peter you don't have to be so graphic.

Look at dis, Peter said, bringing out 24 cards. Credit
cards to da finest stores in Boston and New York. He ain't
so smart.

He has nothing but contempt for you Peter, you and
your kind, why he called politics the hated occupation.

Well he can't think much of me because I'm politics from
foot to head.

He said he didn't want to go the way of the French to
Bonaparte.

Well if you ask me Theda my opinion, I tink some of dees
protestors need a little Bonaparte right up side da fucking
mop baby, pow dat's what dey need.

Now you're cooking with gas Peter, my compatriot and

dear friend. I've been thinking about it Peter and you know what would happen if the British start acting up or them nigger pirates in Barbary start screwing around with our ships. Do we want to look like faggots?

He's stripped the Navy and uses the boats for those old nasty women he's always fooling around with, takes pleasure boat rides with those goddamn anarchists and those pseudo intellectual professors. Why just this morning he took off again. Papers piled high on his desk. Just went away. Too La Doo. Said he was nothing but a lowly dirt farmer waved to us and said he'd see us around. Always using slang like that I can't keep up with him or understand a single thing he says half the time. Said he wanted to catch an eclipse tonight through his telescope. Last time he went to his farm he remained 3 whole months.

Geez dat's a shame Theda. If we had a ballsy leader da whole shebang would be one big goof off from coast to coast, everything would be boss.

Theda looked at himself through a hand mirror and busied the mole on his cheek.

There are plenty of talented men around. Yourself Pete?

O I'm just a poor simple Congressman. I just got da job because my uncle's an undertaker.

Then what about me, Pete? Theda hopped from the crate and clutching the lapels of the Congressman's coat pressed Peter against the wall.

Aw not me, baby, I'm not getting mixed up in no plots.

But your name will become a holiday Peter, just think.

I'd rather bar-be-cue a holiday dan be one Theda. No
tanks. You saw what happened to da Aaron Burr conspiracy, dey busted da poor guy all da way down to da
floor—he's ruined.

Aw Burr was a lemon. I've been secretly planning here in
my little hole in the wall. Maps have been made, an invasion route laid out. Royal Flush Gooseman is extending
credit for supplies in exchange for me sub-leasing Florida
to him, plus I have an intelligence officer on the biggest
cattleman's household staff to boot.

Gee Theda da way you run it down so clear and fresh as
spring water you make it zap my mind.

Of course Peter, dear friend. Why just this evening our
Indian scout out on the range sent a message via electronic
horsey that he was coding Yellow Back Radio when all of a
sudden it went off the beam. He suggests that it might not
be long before I took my sword and led a cavalry charge
on that part of the country full of black diamonds, black
gold, abundant streams of trout and swarming with
healthy steer beef.

Look Theda suppose we just bumped da guy off? I'll let
da boys back home know dere's a contract and while's he's
out looking for rare butterflies bingo poof and my man is
in doornail country.

O Peter you're so sweet but sometimes I forget you're the

Congressman from New Jersey. Assassinations were crude techniques of the Middle Ages. Perish the thought that civilized men like ourselves would be forced to such tactics in this the century of American Enlightenment.

Wipe the mustard off your tie Pete.

O excuse me Theda I didn't notice.

No I have a better plan. If indeed Yellow Back Radio wilting feathers are preparing to take a dive into History why don't we take over the Western section of the country and then declare a civil war? Why with the plentiful resources and cheap labor out there our logistics will be unbeatable and we'd get rid of this crowd once and for all, Hamilton, Paine and Jefferson, the whole civilian crew. Phooey. What do they know. Why I'll be Emperor and Pete . . . well Pete you can park all the stagecoaches. By the way Pete how are things in Congress these days?

O Field Marshal I tink sooner or later we'll get da bakery bilt on da floor of the House. We're wasting money allatime sending out for pies.

I'm just a poor ol snoljer Pete. I mean far be it from me to interfere with the separation of powers but don't you think the fellows ought to put a little hoi-polloi into the proceedings? People are beginning to lose confidence— they'll decide they don't need us and we'll have free stores free money free land—what will happen to our little ego games if anarchy comes about?

A page walked in.

Hey chums there's some redskin out here sez he's got a
message for you. He's out in the lobby with his valet and
tailor.

Thank you page, Theda answered, but in the future please
address us by our rightful titles . . . we're a young country and all but . . .

Up yours, the page replied bringing the forefinger of his
right hand up with a sharp thrust. The page slammed
the door.

Dear, dear, Theda sobbed as Pete screwed on his enor-
mous red nose. Did you see that, they won't even ap-
propriate enough money for me to get a first rate office
staff.

Why do you think da injun's allowed a valet and tailor
Theda?

O he's the last surviving injun in Yellow Back Radio—
Drag Gibson keeps him around in case the Pope wants to
visit or something.

Chief Showcase, representative of red pow wow, was escorted into the room. The Field Marshal looked around
for a chair.

Don't bother gents I'll just sit here on the floor. I know
things are rough for you Field Marshal, having a freaky
bopper peacenik for President and all who has no respect
for the military.

I was on the way back from gay Paree where I bought

this fine Pierre Cardin jacket with fur in the hood and
I wanted to stop off to tell the Field Marshal that signs
point to an early invasion of Yellow Back Radio. Have a
smoke.

O thanks Showcase, here try one Peter dear, the soldier
said handing one to the Congressman.

Cough! Cough! Cough!

The conspirator's mouths became smokestacks as fumes
filled the room.

You know Chief we always regretted the way those rude
Western white trash, that human offal wiped out your
people like that. It was really too bad.

Well Theda if we had had about 50 more troops at Big
Horn I'd be the one sitting on that crate and you'd be
going around the world reading militant poetry, that is
if your ass wasn't on display in some museum.

Yeah, funny da way tings turn out ain't it, Pete said
fidgeting his huge red thumbs and drawing on a cigarette
with two free fingers.

Both Theda and Pete began to be wracked by spasms.

Easy easy gentlemen, Showcase said slapping them on the
back to ease their agony. You must inhale them slowly.

When the two men were finished coughing and spitting
blood Showcase returned to his seat on the floor in the
corner of the room.

Now as I was preparing to report . . . Drag Gibson and the ranch hands were talking about you like a dog. They said they weren't troubled at all about your demand that they join the Union because they knew you didn't have enough troops to make it stick. It was so bad the way they were running you down I cried all the way to Paris.

O isn't that sweet of you, you fine sugar-pappa with the candy between your lucious red thighs. I'll be your little old buffalo calf anytime you want.

Thanks Field Marshal and I'm here to tell you that you and Pete have nothing to fear. Theda something uncanny is happening on the ranch these days. At this very moment some nigger wampus is giving them a run for their money indeed. Cattle are wasting away emitting pitiful moo-moos of mayhem, the fish die on shores and appear in bedrooms in strange flapping monster dances. The darkie even ran the Marshal out of town after a tremendous display of bullwhacking—popped the man with fiery whip-lashes and played songs all over the Marshal's butt so good with his lash that a moose galloped towards a lake and almost drowned, the poor animal was laughing so. And if that wasn't enough the nigger put a hex on John Wesley Hardin and left John Wesley Hardin demented, only fit for tending the hogs.

You mean da famous gunslinger I've read about in da lurid sensational yellow kivered books?

That's the one Pete, the man do nots play—do nots stand for no chump issues. See, he got ringy cause Drag Gibson the cattleman ordered his waddies to burn down a circus troupe the Loop Garoo Kid was hooked up to.

Fact is, gentlemen, Drag is sick now—I don't think he's going to pull through. The local jack-leg squaw on the talk show who gives out the produce market reports and dabbles in astrology shut down her scene. The Kid put some cross on her, had some kind of gris gris dolls placed in her transmitter and the Woman had to sign off and get out of town.

Drag even went and got a mail order bride and it wasn't a week before the Loop Garoo Kid had her running through the mountains in the nude, had done offed with her mind and she was screaming foul nasty things like "make that mojo trigger my snatch one mo time" and mumbling some bad nigger words—you know how they move up and down the line like hard magic beads out riffing all the language in the syntax.

O Red man!! O Red man!! Talk that talk, the Field Marshal said twisting on a crate thrilled to his socks, what jive talking dada you bring us.

Think nothing of it Field Marshal, just hate to see some good cats get a wrong deal. When you going to give me the three colonies?

Soon Showcase soon, if you bring me some more good news like this I'll be polishing my sword and preparing my Army. Sounds like the West is really vulnerable at this point. By the way Injun, from now on call me Theda, Blackwell said, doll circles of pink appearing on the yellow of his jaundiced face.

It's a deal Field Marshal, said the injun rising from the
floor and pulling his cashmere blanket about his shoulders, taking a few puffs from his diamond hookah with a
beaver rimmed mouth piece. Tipping over to the Field
Marshal the savage gave Theda a few taps on the thin
layer of skin covering his coccyx.

By da way Injun if Drag hired John Wesley Hardin da
great Western ghost chaser to get rid of da Kid and Hardin
failed how did Drag have da compassion to keep him on?
I thought Drag had da heart of Two-Pawed Bitch Wolf
of da Plains.

O Drag is still his old name Pete, Showcase responded,
his hand on the door knob and looking over his shoulder. Got a sign above John Wesley Hardin's pigpen
chores—sez for two bits see John Wesley Hardin pay heavy
dues.

O I see, Pete the Peek said as the door was closing behind
Chief Showcase.

One more thing O noble Red man. How will we know when
to move our forces on Yellow Back Radio?

I'll wire you Theda.

Well be sure to wire collect, Pete the Peek said.

No matter Gentlemen I'll pay for it, anything to help out.
In fact Theda here's some money, why don't you go out
and get some new duds? Don't want you to come to your
new Palatinate looking like a bum. Show the cowpokes
you got class.

O no I can't take your Indian Bureau check Chief Showcase.

Never you mind, Theda, you deserve it, the abuse that a
great military mind like yours has to take.

Well if you insist Chief. When Peter and I take over that
territory you'll be set for life. Why you can have your
little happy hunting ground right now here on earth.

I know you'll keep your word you fine white gentlemen,
the Indian said as he walked out of the Field Marshal's
office.

Field Marshal I don't want to dispute what da redman
said, but don't you tink we ought to get a clean white
man in here to give us da facts from da point of view of
Science?

O what were you saying Peter? a blushing Theda Blackwell asked.

O drat it Theda can't you keep your mind on da affairs of
State? With him lost in agrarian reveries and with my
problems (catching flies!), one of us has to keep our
heads.

Your problems Peter?

I've become a very complex freak, Theda baby, Peter
said pulling his pockets inside out. Why I can grope grok
frink—you name it. On da way over here I even learned
to geek. So now I can geek as well as peek.

O Peter with such a crisis mounting don't fun me now
please be serious.

Peter threw up his hands.

Well I guess I have to show you—you asked for it.

Peter went to the control and pressed a button. The
page walked in, a clothespin fastened to his nose. He
carried a chicken by the neck. A real live chicken.

The Page threw the chicken at Pete the Peek who expertly plucked the chicken's feathers and then devoured
the fowl—feathers, coxcomb, gristle, feet disappearing
into his mouth.

Theda looked around for a lavender sink. He was sleepy,
see, and thought he was still at home. He ran to the window and released his insides on passing tourists.

Hey what's going on up dere, buddy, and, you a wise
guy? and other choice Americana expletives rose from
the sidewalk below.

Pete approached Theda with a wishbone.

So you see Theda my problems are very serious and thought
out.

Theda looked around and pulled the larger half of the
bone.

To da conspiracy Theda!!

To the conspiracy Peter!!

A noise was heard at the window. Pete hurriedly put the wishbone into his coat pocket. Harold Rateater, Government Scientist, opened the window and stepped into the room. In one hand he carried a jar filled with smoke and dying insects. He was dressed in a plaid tight-fitting suit and wore a loud bowtie, his hair pasted with staycomb and parted down the middle. He did a mummy-walks-again stride across the room until he stood before Pete and Theda.

My goodness will you please knock next time Harry?

Don't have to Pete, I'm such a smart operator dat I defy da laws of nature. I walk in and out of windows instead of doors. Besides, understand you want to peep through my long glass at dat Loop Garoo Thingamubob unidentified flying phenomenon what's been zooming around.

Please sir! the Field Marshal said, please break it down so that the laity might understand.

In otha words dis is some bad noos for Yellow Back Radio —the Prez ought to be informed at onct—but I got da long glass so what's in it for me? he said gripping the telescope.

Pete was furious. What do you mean what's in it for you? We just appropriated a whole row of iron men so's Dr. Coult could study a rifle dat wouldn't leak gas and get jammed chambers. What more do you guys want?

Theda removed a mallet from his satchel and hit Pete on the head with it. A large lump rose and its peak was immediately occupied by a grey sparrow that flew in through the window.

Ouch! Field Marshal Theda whattaya have to go glunk me on da bean like dat for? the statesman complained.

Forgive Peter, Harold Rateater Government Scientist, he doesn't know any better. Having come up through the ranks he hasn't developed the respect for SCIENCE that a military man like myself has.

Dat's more like it chum, Harold Rateater said, counting the wad of green backs the Field Marshal forked over. Well who wants to look first?

Theda walked over, bent down and looked through the telescope which stuck out of the window.

Field Marshal Theda Blackwell could see into the Cattle Baron's bedroom. He saw the straws in cups of orange juice, the pills, the heavy breathing of Drag Gibson, and his Doctor friend listlessly staring through the window.

O this is too much, Theda said rubbing his frail thin hands together.

Come let me look too dere Theda, I'm da professional voyeur who's suppose to advise and consent like in da constitootion.

Pete the Peek gazed through and it was cookies. Plain cookies.

Yellow Back Radio was indeed falling apart, its batteries were going on the bum, and soon the whole kit and kaboodle would blow a fuse.

● ○

The sheep are happier of themselves, than under the care of wolves.

Thomas Jefferson

Meanwhile back at the ranch Chief Showcase entered Drag's sick room. The old fat and ignorant cattlerancher lay in bed, his chest rapidly rising and falling. The Dr. was seated next to the window, his head in his hands as he did vigil for his old friend. Whispering, he saluted the Indian.

O Chief Showcase how loyal of you to come see Drag. Why just a few minutes ago we found some horrible material stuffed in his pillow. It was made up of putrid matter I analyzed to be: a one-eyed toad, wings of a bat, cat's eyes and some strange powder. Things look grave indeed.

Chief Showcase gently sat on Drag's bed and put a hand on the Cattleman's forehead. Drag's eyebrows fluttered. The room was spinning as his eyes opened.

O Chief Showcase, he said weakly, good of you to come and visit me before I ride off into the eternal sunset.

Think nothing of it Drag, I was on my way back from Paris and I stopped off at that makeshift acreage they call the Capitol.

Even in his dying spasms Drag laughed as did the Doc,

who beamed at the Indian for bringing a little humor into the room.

I overheard them talking about you Drag and it surprised me seeing as how any fool could tell that you are in charge, the top dog and the one who is really number 1.

O thanks sweet Redman, Drag said clasping the Indian's hand, but looks like Drag is about to enter the Great Corral in the Sky.

That's what they were saying Drag. They said they might raise a cavalry and investigate those mysterious wife deaths. They said you might fill up boot hill quicker than you think. They said you called them corny dudes and all but at least back East they either kills niggers or prizes them to death. Here sign this autograph.

Drag obliged, scratching a feeble signature on a scrap of paper provided by the Indian.

Well they ain't no threat, even in my dying breath I know that Unification it'll never happen. Why I understand that the largest bank in the country is out in this territory now.

The door opened. A messenger ran into the room and handed Drag a note. Drag's eyes popped. He sat up in bed and slapped his hand against his forehead.

Now I get it. Of course. Too much. That's it. Me getting sick and the cattle dying like that. Yeah of course. Now it makes sense. Hot diggity joe joe—won't be long now—

The Indian and the Doctor were amazed at this rapid recovery by one who only a few moments before had taken out a passport for the beyond. Whatever the contents of this note—it provided a powerful curative.

What's wrong Drag, what happened, they asked him eagerly.

A note from the Pope. It won't be long now. Everybody take off his hat. Imagine that—I am nothing but a lowly cattleman, ugly fat and ignorant, why I use to slop hogs and ride drag, that's why they call me Drag, because my first job was taking care of back tracking and sick cattle. But now—a royal visit!

Drag leaped out of bed and in his nightgown and cap ran past the Indian and into the hall. Below the men were making bets on his hour of departure. They scooped up their money when they saw the boss at the top of the stairs . . .

Men, things are really going to change now—tomorrow all the way from Rome the Pope is arriving to straighten out this inner sanctum mystery once and for all. Hang out some confetti, get the fiddler, round up all the hurdy gurdy girls from the Rabid Black Cougar—a big huzza huzza time.

Everybody made eager preparations for the visit. Banners were hung over the street, ikons strategically placed, the whole town was incensed. And everyone was engaged in furious preparations for the Pope's visit. Everyone, that is, but Chief Showcase, who was sneaking towards the Hotel to send off a telegram.

● ○

Wooooooo weell Um ma um ma um ma ha hall Su ha
su ha su hall Soo-kee o soo-kee soo-kee. Lalalalalalalala
lalalalalalalala. My my my my goodness. O get it. Get
it
GET IT GET IT OOOOOOOOOooooooooooooooooooo
oooo oooo
o   o   *time* Mewwwwooooooooooow.

Your charm certainly works. Your strong black hands just
seem to make my bones jump and shout for joy. Please
ask the owner for my car keys. You can come to my
apartment and take anything you want. Take my credit
cards, take my status—it doesn't mean anything just do
it to me more often, you know how you do things so fine
and sweet. You the finest pipe fitter I've ever known, O I
just wish I could do more to reward you for your thrilling
expertise.

Can we say sex?

The Field Marshal nestled his head next to the black
masseur's thighs as he lay in semi-consciousness on the
table of an underground rub down Palace in the basement of the Army's headquarters.

Think nothing of it boss-man Theda, the masseur said,
you know I'll do my bit to help relax you in these troubled
times. The ship of state needs strong arms at its oars now
don't it.

O you're so beautiful and understanding. Theda's eyes became moist as he closed in on the black man and started to purr like a kitten.

Mee-yow, mee-yow, he purred while the masseur softly stroked his back. O I think I'll just go out of my mind if you start sucking my toes like you did last week, Theda said.

The pink mist of the room was heavily perfumed and across the area on other tables, high ranking members of the Army were babbling softly out of their minds while big black masseurs in turbans and baggy pants were running their jazzy hands across their bodies.

You know, sweet and ample black man, I tried to get that provision in the Declaration of Independence, a forthright resolution, but nothing happened. The Southern planters were dead set against it and we needed their support.

I know, Theda, I read the broadsides, I know you did all you could. Me and my wife have a picture of you on our wall. Each morning we light candles fo it and pray fo you and Mr. Thomas Jefferson. He's a good man too.

Tom's all right, Theda said, but he's such a rake, nothing but a dirt farmer and anarchist. Hangs out with Jacobins like that Paine fellow. I've even seen him out with women from time to time. And he doesn't know how to keep his britches on at all. Some man in Conn. is suing him for adultery right now and he reads French books and plays electric fiddle with some rock group called the Green Mountain Boys. O he's disgusting sometimes.

Well suh, the masseur said, his hands pressing against
Theda's neck, causing him to wiggle, what about Ben-
jamin Franklin?

O he's just as bad, he and that Westerner Henry Clay,
they carry on—Franklin draws cartoons—he invented
balloon speech you know. And that Clay always brawling.
Me and the fellows tried to get Randolph of Virginia to
head the Convention but he was overruled. Some dele-
gate with a squirrel cap and a filthy backwoods buckskin
jacket on spread the word that Randolph was second rate
at what jackasses could do infinitely better—o democracy
sometimes. Phew.

Big Woogie?

Yes Theda?

What about this Hoo . . . this religion the Hoo-Doo that
your people practice?

Big Woogie stepped back. Some of the other black attendants started to roll their eyes and drop their towels.
Confusion broke out as the members of the Army asked
their attendants to continue massaging their tired bones.
Snapping his fingers, Big Woogie gave them the signal to
return to their work.

O it's nothing Theda, nothing to get upset about. Just some
kind of superstition that our people brought from Africa.
People believe in hants and such things, that's all.

O I see, the Field Marshal said.

The page, now wearing his Hoover's cap and knicker-bockers, walked into the room.

Hey fuck-face Doompussy, whatever your name is.

Theda jumped from the table.

Well I never. Who gave you this address? I told them to never give out this phone number—why this is one of the few luxuries I have in this life . . .

Aw be quiet, the page said. I just came to give you this telegram that just arrived.

Theda went into one of the phone booths for privacy, his bathrobe still wrapped about him. He slapped his knees and gave a great hoot when he read the telegram's contents.

> *Drag is about to tip away.*
> *The whole thing belongs to you baby.*
> *Come on in your Highness.*
>
> Showcase

V. A Jigsaw Of A Last Minute Rescue

The Pope rode on a loud red bull in front of a great stagecoach full of attendants, with footmen on each side. The bull wore a garland of hyacinths around his neck. The people of Yellow Back Radio, still high out of their minds from devil's pills and accustomed to fantasy in their lives, stood on the sidelines and cheered for this gigantic whopper now appearing before them.

All the notables stood in front of Big Lizzy's Rabid Black Cougar to greet the Pope. Big Lizzy held a bouquet of violets, ignoring the scorn of the town's women, standing on the sidelines.

The Banker stood next to Drag and Doc. He had made an honorary batch of traveler's checks with the Pope's picture on them.

⟶ further mockery

Only Rev. Boyd was missing. He was in the saloon sucking like a champ. He felt that Drag had double crossed him when he promised that Protestantism would last at least a month and there was only a day or so to go and here Drag was greeting some foreign discipline.

No children in sight, the Pope distributed pennies to the townsfolk. The people scrambled about in the dust for them, except for those too mind blown to move, who just stood on the sidelines and clapped while answering the Father's waves with:

Work out, Pope. You got the business! Rap, Pope! Run down strong things and be as savvy as you always have been.

When the procession stopped in front of the Rabid Black Cougar, Drag Gibson stepped down and handed the Pope a welcome-to-our-city gift:

On behalf of the citizens of Yellow Back Radio, I give to you this jumbo-size cheeseburger.

The Pope smiled indulgently, although he turned up his nose and ordered one of his footmen to take charge of the big beef between two half-done buns.

The people applauded.

Thank-a you citizens of Yellow Back Radio. I'm-a come to cool tings out and get rid of this maleficiem what's been making the cattle break out in sores, their milk to dry, that's parching your fields with-a plague—in other words howdy pardners before I'm-a adios everything will be really really fine as wine in the summertime.

Wow, everybody said, what a showman this Pope is, man-o-man.

Drag curtsied and fell flat on his face. Everyone laughed while the men helped him out of the dirt and brushed off his clothes. In the prevailing good mood Drag chuckled along with the peasants.

We're going to make your visit very enjoyable Pope. How long you want to stay in Yellow Back? The town is yours.

I have-a no time to tarry, the Pope said looking at the pocket watch he brought from underneath his gown.

Drag tried to remove the skull cap the Pope wore on his head. The Pope started to slap Drag around the arms. Get you cotton pickin hands off my head!

O I'm sorry I was just trying to make your visit comfortable. Well Pope we'll take you and your coachmen footmen and aides up to the ranch where we can all have a big celebration tonight.

● ○

At the celebration the Pope sat on a throne Drag had made for him. Drag sat next to him looking important. Whenever the Pope leaned over and whispered into his ear, he would look on to the proceedings knowingly, making a circle with his thumb and forefinger as if he had been privy to secret knowledge.

A commotion was caused in front of the door near the garden. Suddenly it opened. The preacher stood in its well. Iridescent wings annexed to his shoulders were flapping and his eyes were bugged. His tail was ignited with electricity. The Preacher started across the floor towards the Pope. The Pope's aide brought a giant can of DDT and the Pope started to squish. The Preacher grabbed his neck and stumbled back. He keeled over with his feet up and his wings oscillated until they were still. Never again would it oviposit eggs.

I'm-a sorry I had to do that to one of your dignitaries, Pope said to the Drag.

O that's all right Father. He tried his best but Protestant-ism was the heathen German's reaction to the glory of Rome. He was bound to go all atavistic sooner or later. Besides this was no costume party anyway. We is big time and serious.

Glad you understand Drag, the Pope said while people gathered around the Preacher on the floor.

Where can we talk about this Loop-a Garoo Kid?

Why is this his accent?

Now you're talking there Father, Drag said, come on into my study.

The men went upstairs, the cowpokes stomping their boots so as to impress the hurdy gurdy girls they brought from Big Lizzy's on how they had access to high places.

Upstairs the Pope had an aide roll out a map while he held a pointer. It was a diagram of Yellow Back Radio.

Do you know where he's hiding out?

No, that's just it, the Drag said, there are so many caves around here he could be hiding out in who could tell. Why the night he came to our party there the men fear-lessly rode after him and they couldn't find him. Right, men?

The foreman looked on as the other men lowered their heads. Right Drag, that's what we did. We almost had him but couldn't catch up.

Snow is the ticket, the Pope said, removing a cigar from his gown pocket and lighting up.

What happened to your final A's there Pope?

Shit, man! That's for suckers. Me and you cattlemen are in the same bag, always have been, moolas where it's at, look at that Sistine. Whatdaya think bilt that dump. Cheese? The mob loves final A's, them Protestants they never know, no ritual no class, so that when a generation of kids came along who could concentrate on more than one thing at a time they couldn't handle it.

The Pope's aide was handing out cigars and the men, leaning back in their chairs, laughed at one another while pulling forward their suspenders.

That was no threat for us. We hand out them wafers, and swing them censers, lot of loud singing, organs, processions. They like it that way.

That's the way I was running things Pope, till this nigger come in here and turned the place out.

Well we'll see about him—when we were threatened by the Albigenses, the Waldenses and other anarchists way back there when we couldn't absorb them we burned or hanged them. Where was I? the Pope continued.

You were talking about caves.

Look for the Peak of No Mo Snow, Drag. He hates snow.

Why I seed a naked mountain top just the other day, Skinny said. Let's go boys.

The men rose and were about to head for the hills when the Pope cautioned them:

Hold it, hold it, you don't go in there with your cowboy thing like that—shoot-em-ups won't work this time. He's got power stored in that mad dog's tooth hanging on that necklace he wears. The mad dog's tooth is the thing.

You have to find some way to remove it from his neck. Then he's powerless. In Haiti it's called an arret but here in America it's liable to be named anything. America is such a strange place that according to the new occult dictionary that just arrived at the Vatican Library there are more queer sects here than anywhere in the world. The religions turn out to be as rag-time a collage as the American Episcopalians who received their charter from a heretical Irish group.

Just for the record Father, Drag asked, what is he putting on us anyhow?

Well we've figured it to be the Hoo-Doo, an American version of the Ju-Ju religion that originated in Africa—you know, that strange continent which serves as the sub-conscious of our planet—where we've found the earliest remains of man. Ju-Ju originated in Dahomey and Angola. You'll find that wangol, one of the magical terms of the system, is a play on that country's name.

Who knows what lurks in the secret breast of that Continent, shaped so like the human skull? We've tried to hide the facts by ridiculing the history of Sub-Sahara Africa and claiming that of North Africa as our own. Notice how the term "blackamoor" was dropped from St. Augustine's name, and how our friends the German Aryan scholars faked the History of the Egyptians by claiming them to be white. Have you ever seen any examples of their art? If you just look at the pictures—the way they painted themselves black—and ignore the propaganda in our texts or Nefertiti which is a fraud, you will find that undoubtedly they are black people. The overwhelming majority of their art depicts black people.

Sometimes I suspect that if Eve had remained in that garden, probably located in Dahomey, because that's where the snakes are, Rome would be merely one of the centers of the Ju-Ju religion and I'd be nothing but a poor wretch, stomping grapes or directing traffic in New York City.

The men were falling asleep. Drag stood and fired into the ceiling. Wake up you guys, have a little respect for the Vatican.

Well anyway, the Pope continued, when African slaves were sent to Haiti, Santo Domingo and other Latin American countries, we Catholics attempted to change their pantheon, but the natives merely placed our art alongside theirs. Our insipid and uninspiring saints were no match for theirs: Damballah, Legba and other dieties which are their Loa. This religion is so elastic that some of the women priests name Loa after their boyfriends.

When Vodun arrived in America, the authorities became so paranoid they banned it for a dozen or so years, even to the extent of discontinuing the importation of slaves from Haiti and Santa Domingo.

Loop Garoo seems to be practicing a syncretistic American version. I'll bet you've found ugly matter in your pillows, dolls on the door steps, maybe a personal item of clothing and a portrait of yourself missing.

It's important that we wipe it out because it can always become a revolutionary force. Many of the Haitian revolutionaries were practicing priests, or houngans, as they are called. The present Prime Minister of Haiti Dr. François Duvalier was former head of the Haitian Bureau of Ethnology.

Loop seems to be scatting arbitrarily, using forms of this and adding his own. He's blowing like that celebrated musician Charles Yardbird Parker—improvising as he goes along. He's throwing clusters of demon chords at you and you don't know the changes, do you Mr. Drag?

Father you let us handle this guy.

May I make a suggestion?

What is it Pope?

Does he have any close friends or companions?

Now that you mention it Pope, I think that I did see him ride off from here last night and join two men who

were waiting for him on the hill, said Skinny McCullough
the foreman.

Then get 10 dollars and a bottle of wine plus two tickets
to the East on the Black Swan Stagecoach. Those men
will remove the mad dog's tooth from the necklace he
wears around his neck, the source of his power. They're
probably down and out artists. He always liked artists.

O Pope you don't believe in all that mumbo jumbo do
you? I mean you're a swell conversationalist but come
off of it Pope.

The Pope looked at Drag in disgust. One should always
believe the other side is capable of doing anything it says
—you're a young country and you don't know that but
you'll learn—the hard way.

Just to placate the Pope, Drag gave the men a bottle of
cheap dirty wine, 2 stagecoach tickets and a rolled-up
10 dollar bill. And they were off to find the Peak of No
Mo Snow.

● ○

When they reached the Loop Garoo's hideout, the Peak
of No Mo Snow, Skinny put his finger to his lips, a
signal for the horsemen to shush and kneel behind the
foliage some yards from the cave. The hours passed and
the sun settled behind the hills.

The gang's patience was rewarded because it wasn't long

before Alcibiades Wilson and Jeff Williams emerged from the cave's mouth.

Man, you know, Jeff, Alcibiades said, if a cat laid 10 dollars on me, a bottle of wine and a ticket on the Black Swan Stagecoach for the East I'd split in a jiffy. We can return to the cafes and just be throwing our mops against the walls and be boo-ga-looing until our hearts' content.

You said it Alcibiades, I would do it too. The Kid is really got the coo-coo fever. Having ceremonies with that snake, saying those curses and drawing funny scenes on the cave's wall; extinct creatures and cattle in a head-on collision. If we can get to the East we'll be just in time to do some macking at the Washington Square Art Show.

Skinny McCullough walked out of the bush whistling with his hands behind his back. The two men, seated on a rock outside of the cave and smoking cigarettes, almost knocked each other over trying to run back into the hideout.

Hold on, hold on there men, you've nothing to fear from me, why I'm nothing but a broken down hermit, given to such eccentricities as supporting artists and collecting roots. I live around these parts and just came over to comment on how much I like your aquiline noses. You kids really look smart there, I mean those thin lips, you look like some of them Roman statoots.

You really think so? answered Alcibiades. Why I played Puck in the Central Park production of *Midsummer's Night Dream*.

Me too!! Me too!! Jeff echoed. I've played Puck plenty of times.

You boys ought to go to New York and become artists and writers—I'll bet you'd be a hot hit right off.

That's what we were just saying, mister, we said if we had a bottle of wine, two tickets on the Black Swan Stagecoach, we'd be off for the East right away. We're being held captive by a mad man who wears a mad dog's tooth about his neck and talks crazy.

Is that so? Skinny answered. Why it just so happens I'm a collector of mad dogs' teeth. I need one more to round out my hobby. You think your friend there will give it to me?

Man, no good, Alcibiades answered, he plays with it all the time and never removes it from about his neck.

Skinny started to walk away but said over his shoulder, Gee that's too bad. I was going to give him a bottle of wine, two tickets back East and some fast finnifs.

Jeff and Alcibiades conferred rapidly as Skinny started down Peak's path.

Hey mister!! Wait a minute!! I don't think the Kid would mind if you borrowed it for a while. He's asleep right now but we'll go in and ask him.

Now you're talking, Skinny said, I'll wait right here.

The men lit torches and entered the cave. When they came

upon the area where Loop Garoo was asleep they stole towards him and gently removed the necklace from around Loop's neck. The white python glared from his cage above the altar.

Alcibiades and Jeff crept away while Loop watched with one eye open. He chuckled to himself as the men headed out of the cave and into the night where Skinny was waiting. They extinguished the torches.

O.K., said Alcibiades panting like a puppy, suh, heah's yo mad dog's tooth.

Skinny examined the mad dog's tooth through a magnifying glass. Excellent!! Excellent!! Thank you gentlemen, and here is the filthy half-full bottle of muscatel wine in an ol beat up dirty sack, the tickets on the stagecoach and some finnifs for your trouble, Skinny said throwing the items at their feet.

Alcibiades started to fight with Jeff over the wine while Skinny leaned back and laughed heartily.

When they finished the bottle they picked up the tickets and money and ran down the hill towards Yellow Back Radio to fetch the coach.

They ran so hard that every few steps they leaped into the air like chickens.

Skinny walked to the bushes where the men were giggling over the scene they had just witnessed.

All right men, Skinny said, let's go get this black berserk

who thinks he's a buckaroo. We'll show him a thing or two.

The men spat into their hands and, lighting torches, started into the cave.

The cowpokes descended, holding the flares in their hands until they came upon an opening where Loop Garoo lay, pretending to be asleep.

Gotcha now!! Gotcha now!! Raise your hands you frightening coon you!! Start grabbing the blue. You ain't so tough, cause you lost the mad dog's tooth from around your neck. Now we understand them dolls we found on the boss's doorstep every morning, making him sick, and the rooster with the top hat and tails. The goat without horns makes a lot of sense now, a lot of sense.

Them artists you've been holding captive, they took the thing and gave it to us and the Pope of the Romans—he snitched to us about what you were up to.

So the Pope told you of my connaissance huh? Loop asked sitting up from the cave floor.

Reach for the sky and don't be smart.

How's the Pope these days?

What, insolent nigger, you trying to question Rome or something? Skinny yelled, knocking the Loop Garoo to the ground. Get up and start marching.

They tied Loop's hands and began to shove him out of the cave.

He looked back to the altar. Then above to the cage. The cage was open and the snake was nowhere to be seen. Loop looked over to a dark pool on the other side of the cave and saw a white tail disappearing into the water.

I said move on Loop, keep movin, the foreman said, as he and the cowpokes took their prisoner to Yellow Back Radio.

● ○

The hump-backed attendant was tormenting the Loop by dangling a grey mouse before him. He would rush forward with the dead rodent on a string and push it through the bars. As soon as Loop was about to knock the stick down the attendant would quickly retreat laughing.

Loop, impatient with the antics, was about to turn the little man into stone—having had it up to his ears with Yellow Back Radio—when he heard a commotion outside the cell block.

The Pope walked into the corridor of the prisoner's section. Other prisoners, when they saw the visitor, banged their coffee mugs against the bars.

Wow, the pin-headed attendant shouted when he saw the Pope. He ran up to the Pope and began kissing him all

over his hands. Moof, moof, Pope, wait until I tell my
mother about seeing you, moof, moof—let me hold your
train.

The Pope stroked the attendant's back and it became
straight. The attendant skipped about the room, then
returned and kissed the Pope's hands with even greater
passion.

O.K. little attendant, let's not get carried away now, take
the rest of the day off—I want to be alone with this sinner.

You sure you don't need me Pope? He's a tough hombre,
the attendant said, snarling at Loop.

I can handle him little attendant. Now you go off and
fall into the first well you see.

Anything you say Father, the attendant said, running out
of the block.

What do you want Innocent? Loop asked as soon as they
were alone. Isn't it enough that you turned me in?

The Pope drew his skirts up around him and folded his
hands glowing with huge rings.

Look Loop you know me, I wouldn't have done anything
if it hadn't been for the woman. She wants you to come
back Loop. Ever since her ascension she's been with
the blues. T. S. Eliot, one of those trembling Anglicans,
said "blue is her color." But now it's her song and her day.
Those other two, they behave as if they had ice cubes up
their asses.

The raunchy Pope, Loop grinned, you were always my favorite. What did they say of you?

> *eight boys eight girls*
> *the Pope in sinful love begat*
> *Rome him "father" rightly calls*

Cut it out Loop. Why don't you give up this nonsense and come back home?

Loop ignored the Pope's request and looked distantly out of his cell window.

How did you find me?

Wasn't hard—mass murder, sexual excess, drugs, dancing, music. It was quite simple. We used the Vatican dirigible and circled the Valley until we spotted the Peak of No Mo Snow. After all Loop, in these many years we have come to know you as well as the back of our left hands.

You've got your nerve. What about the Witches' Hammer that you and the ol man cooked up to crush my followers way back when? When you and your cronies finished it was so bad that in some villages only a few women could be found alive.

O Loop let sleeping dogs lie. Anyway I'm here to question you, not you me.

As always—Inquisition Inquisition. I would venture to guess that your Inquisition signaled the triumph of the

clerk, the bureaucrat, and the West has been in the com-
mittee thing ever since.

Loop you know you could have leveled this town with
a word. We were observing you. We looked it up in the
Book of Mysteries and found what you were doing with
the snake and the charms. We thought we'd play along
with you. Of course the ol man wanted us to come blasting like before, you know how ill tempered he is—belliger-
ent chariot fleets, thunder storms, earthquakes. But she
overruled him, gave him a headache. At times it seems
she's about to take over. Loop, we figured out your game,
what's your point?

Horse opera. Clever don't you think? And the Hoo-Doo
cult of North America. A much richer art form than
preaching to fishermen and riding into a town on the
back of an ass. And that apotheosis. How disgusting. He
had such an ego. "I'm the Son of God." Publicity hound,
he had to prolong it for three hours, just because the press
turned out to witness. And his method had no style at
all. Compare his cheap performance at the gravesight of
Lot—sickening—and that parable of our friend Buddha
and the mustard seed. One, just a grandstand exhibition,
and the other, beautiful, artistic and profound.

Like Father like Son always, getting hang-ups in the way
of craftsmanship. Nails, driven into the wrist, hypocritical
and maudlin women. Why she was screaming at his feet
for three hours and the next night in my room I thought
she would bite off my horns with the steel of her hungry
teeth. Two weeks later I had her on the block and rolling
bums. She even attracted two other tricks, and I had a
family. It was groovy until that angel he sent—the im-

postor who spread the rumor of her ascension and before you knew it—it became a Papal Dogma.

She went uptown on me and left me holding the bag—and as soon as she left, Mighty Dike and Mustache Sal mustered enough courage to leave too.

You're his Son too, Loop.

Yes, the eldest according to what they call apocrypha. You know how his propagandists are—anything they disapprove of they ascribe to hearsay, apocrypha or superstition. But I've never cashed in on it like he did. I knew very early that he wasn't the only one, there were others —but his arrogance and selfishness finally got the best of him and he drove them all underground. Now they're making a strong comeback.

So you're through with this performance, huh Loop?

Yes, even martyrdom can be an art form, don't you think? Hoo-doo, which in America flowered in New Orleans, was an unorganized religion without ego-games or death worship. In the States, books like the *6th & 7th Books of Moses, The Art of Burning Candles, The Explanation of Voo-Dooism, Mystic Secrets of Mind and Power, Egyptian Secrets of Albertus Magnus,* or *White and Black Art for Man & Beast,* are sold across the counter at drugstores. I even had a betrayal motif, giving one upmanship on his most obvious forms.

You always did dig artists Loop, in the old days passing the elixir to those writers and painters in the cafe, pretending to be a patron.

Loop reflected. Remember when he came home that day Innocent? The old man made love to him as if they were man and wife. He licked his punctures and fed him from the breast.

So you think by allowing yourself to be humiliated by mortals he'll respect you too, huh?

No I just wanted to show the world what they were really up to. I'm always with the avant-garde. Seems to me that people are getting sick of daddies. You know—"thou shalt have no other before me"—Tsars, Monarchs, and their deadly and insidious flunkies.

Loop, one last time before you get on your soap box. He wants you to come home too—she's driving them batty. O Loop she's so bitchy, you know how she is. He even put a curse on her but she found a way to absorb that. Matter of fact she's getting a following up there. Both of them are afraid she might start something that'll make your uprising look quite small.

There was never an uprising, Innocent, you know that. That was some of his propagandists in the late Middle Ages who came up with that idea. Just got sick of that set-up and left. The fool—vagabond with the rucksack on my shoulder—always on the road. That's me, the cosmic jester. Matter of fact, I've always been harmless—St. Nick coming down the chimney, children leaving soup for me—always made to appear foolish, the scapegoat of all history. You and your crowd are the devils. The way you massacred the Gnostics, not to mention the Bogomils, Albigenses, and Waldenses.

Loop, he sent me to do the interrogating . . . I ask you one more time Loop, end this foolishness and come on home. He built a special district for you, red lights, the works. He sent for some of your bohemian types to keep you and Diane company. You can start a commune if you want, get high, walk around nude, anything you want Loop, just so you satisfy the wench.

No dice, baby.

O.K., Loop, the worldly Pope said rising, I should know that when you have your mind made up on something, nothing can change it. When I get back he's really going to put me down.

How's that?

Makes me crawl on *my* belly toward him and kiss *his* feet. Some days Loop I can't stand the place. People singing the same old hymns and he sits there performing the familiar spectaculars—every day. I miss St. Peter's chug-a-lugging fine brandy with the gang and jamming some strumpets.

Sorry, can't help you out Innocent, I told the bitch to stay. I almost went out of my mind to suicide, but she went on. As they say, or as he use to say when he tried to con the farmers, pretending he was one of their own, "as ye sow so shall ye reap."

● ○

The Pope's mission a failure, he left the jailhouse and climbed into the waiting carriage to start the long journey home. Since there was no further need to impress the people of the town, the red bull had been flown out the night before to the ship waiting for the Vatican party.

Sulking, Drag walked to the window of the carriage.

Well Father, too bad you can't stay for one of our old fashioned lynchings that we Americans love so much and that's a traditional source of entertainment. Why the hangman just ordered some new gadget special all the way from France for the killing this time. But since you can't stay, as a token of our appreciation and for "enlightening" us here's another gift—a plastic hot dog, one foot long, that grew in a swamp in the basement of Kresge's. How's about that shit, your Pontiff?

The Pope contemptuously knocked the hot dog from Drag's hand. Not only was he upset by Drag's choice of word "enlightening," but when he got home with the bad news everybody would start crying the blues. Whole choirs for days on end.

You idiot slob, I didn't come here to kill the Loop Garoo Kid, I came to draw him out, to talk to him. If you think you can do away with him then you Americans are stupider meatheads than the rest of the world gives you credit.

Onward! The Pope snapped his fingers and his caravansary started to roll towards the mountains on its way to the dock.

Drag's face was long and glum.

Cheer up, Drag, Skinny McCullough said putting his arm about his boss's shoulder.

Well at least he came to visit. But I guess I'll have to change my deodorant. He behaved as if . . . well as if my armpits had bad breath. *∪ — Like the end of a sitcom*

● ○

Loop Garoo was led from the jail a few hours later. The townsfolk were too cool to jeer.

Drag climbed to the scaffold and, swaying with a bottle of 3X's in his hand, shoved the part-time trainer and hangman aside. The hangman shrugged his shoulders and removed his black hood. He checked in the time clock on the ground next to the steps and then started home. As long as the execution was performed the Union would see that he got paid. Plus they'd give him a bonus for his suggestion—the guillotine that he had imported to *Reed is very anti-American* spice things up a bit. He was a typical American worker—what's in it for me was written all over the guy's face.

Drag was reading the instructions on the brand new device while the men held Loop Garoo on the platform. The treacherous swine behind the scaffold were tying linen around their necks and held forks in their hooves, so eager were the foul beasts for the poor devil's head to fall.

Drag swaggered about the scaffold with drops of liquor

dripping from the bottle, and some of it running from the corners of his mouth.

Aw this is taking too long. Let's go home and get high, said one citizen.

Yeah this is corny old fashioned junk anyway, another one responded.

What did you say? Did my ears hear me right? Drag yelled, reeling about the platform as he threw the bottle into the onions, mustard and pickles which littered the area in front of the platform where the Pope had refused his gift.

You want to abandon American institutions, huh!! When you give up your institutions, you ain't got nothin someone once said. Get back here and watch this good old killing. Make em get up their hands, boys.

The cowpokes stared at the crowd behind their sunglasses and menacingly placed their hands on their holsters.

Where are my servants? I want them to be in on this too, Drag shouted.

They ain't here, Chief Showcase called from behind the crowd, just me and my blankets. The chinaboy was seen heading towards the lake last night with an armful of blueprints of your tomb. There was a neck topped with a huge revolving eye protruding from the water.

Well I don't need no tomb anyway, now that I've been clued in by the Pope on what was going down in me.

Loop, what you got to say, Drag said holding the blade's brake as his men shoved Loop's head to the chopping block.

How do you like this parody on his passion, you old Codger, Loop said staring skyward.

Everyone got a chuckle out of that and even Loop smiled as Drag started to send the blade to split his head from his torso. The hogs behind the scaffold began to pant loud and rude.

All at once the white Chicken Delight truck pulled up to the rear of the crowd with two surviving Yellow Back children swinging from its doors. Their mouths were full of drumsticks. Hey come on, we found it, the Seven Cities of Cibola! It's as far as you can see from where you're standing now.

The common folk turned away from the scaffold and sure enough there in the distance could be seen rising a really garish smaltzy super technological anarcho-paradise. The people began to trot in slow motion towards the blue kidney shaped swimming pools, the White Castle restaurants, the drive-in bonanza markets, the computerized buses and free airplanes, the free anything one desired.

 O no, Loop complained, not another medieval morality drama with me getting the wooden paddle in the tail at the end.

Hold on, grab them Drag, the lush shouted to his gang.

the kids

The cowpokes blocked the people's progress. Some of them drew shooting irons, others squirted the townsfolk with mace.

If there's some kind of Cibola place what's got exploitative possibilities I'm going to be the one to get the coin. Why I'll be a squillionaire.

Aw come off it Drag, one of the children swinging from the Chicken Delight truck yelled, act normal will ya?

The townsfolk booed Drag, some of them giving him the razzberry, others the bird.

Throw the bum out, they screamed pinching their noses.

A cavalry charge sounded. It was the Government arriving in an invasion fleet of taxis around the bend and into the town.

Theda Blackwell leaped from the lead auto and was about to read a hastily written decree to the crowd when he saw Drag looking robust and swaying on the scaffold. He nervously glanced at Showcase to the rear of the crowd for an explanation but Chief Showcase shrugged his shoulders giving the Theda a what-do-you-want-from-me-already type stare and returned to munching on an ice cream sandwich one of the children had given him.

Very well, Theda said. Drag Gibson in the name of the Queen I place you and your men under arrest.

The Field Marshal was dressed like a Dresden Doll. His wig had been curled dressed and talcumed. His cheeks and lips were tinted. He wore a tiny patch of black court plaster on his face. Gold lace decorated the sleeves of his wine colored frock coat. He wore white stockings which reached his knees and evening pumps.

All of Drag's bulldoggers rolled about in the dust, they were laughing so at this tenderfoot coming out of the blue.

Theda's earrings shook slightly as he summoned the rest of his party: Pete the Peek and his sleuths who wore trench coats and black slouch hats.

O funny huh, said Theda. Yes I know that you in the West think we're panty-waist style and we may be by your standards, but don't forget we're the ones with the Industrial Revolution. Take em, boys.

The sleuths behind them turned their rat noses and meat cleaver jaws towards the Skinny McCullough and the rest of the men from the Purple Bar-B.

Ray Guns!!!

The cowpokes tried to draw but they were no match for Harold Rateater's latest toy. Sheath after sheath of strange lights flashed on their bodies and they melted slowly into a pile of goo.

Drag was pop-eyed, standing on the scaffold and tottering.

We'll settle this your way, we'll show you that we're gentlemen, Drag Gibson.

Suits me fine, Drag said. I may be a little rusty but I'm sure I can outdraw you.

The Field Marshal and Drag began to pace backwards but suddenly Drag's arms were moving like windmills as he tried to balance himself on the edge of the platform. He disappeared into the little yard behind this grim stand.

Noisy and much munching was heard from the greedy and unnatural animals who dwelled there.

The Field Marshal flanked by Pete and his stooges started once again to read the decree annexing Yellow Back Radio to the East.

Suddenly spears flew from the summit of the Mountain overlooking Yellow Back Radio.

The sleuths, Pete the Peek and Theda, groaning, tried to remove the spearheads deeply buried in their chests. Soon men lay wasted in the streets. They resembled the scribblings of little children—sticks for arms and circles for heads.

Wow! said the cabbies.

Gee whiz! said the townsfolk. The Government is been wiped out.

Revolution   Communist — last of line book

That's what we've been trying to tell you all along, said the children. Come on, let's go, the late late late show is about to begin on the boob toob and we can watch eating Pooped Out Soggies.

What happens to Loop?

Everyone arm in arm started bopping towards the gleaming Cities in the distance. Some even slopped, and a few solid sender old timers who could remember broke out into some very heavy trucking. Theda's page trailed along doing the camel walk.

Big Lizzy shared a two-seated bicycle with Chief Showcase.

They all ignored the Loop Garoo Kid left standing on the scaffold and cheated out of his martyrdom. He watched the crowds disappear in the clouds of dust. He climbed down from his prospective punishment ignoring the hogs, whose jaws were swollen with Cattleman à la carte.

He rode rapidly over the Mountain and off into the distance in an effort to catch up with the Pope's ship.

At the summit of the Mountain husky women with stubs for left breasts were putting their remaining spears into pouches made from hides of oxen.

The Amazons watched the mob working out joyfully towards the futuristic scenes in the distance. All along the way black flags furled in the breeze. They sat on their horses and some prepared the dayglo paint which circled their eyes. You would think that these women, barefooted and clothed in leopard skin, having just left the neolithic, would be more than glad to go off to where machines were servants and could do everything from dig irrigation ditches to baby sitting—where even old people were free to watch the movies since machines would from now on change diapers, where engines punched in instead of men.

The Amazons preferred their own thing. It was a big world wasn't it? And who cared as long as no one starved and everybody could swing the way he wanted.

The Amazons rode back to their forests. Having disposed of certain biological accidents they would have a celebration tonight. There would be much wine drunk, dancing and messages to be sent out to other liberated tribes.

● O

Hey Matthew, said one pig to his greedy and carnivorous companion who was nibbling the plumes of a Napoleon hat.

What do you want Waldo?

Pretty good week here for us pigs ain't it?

Yeah guys. First that tomato topped with the rose and then this fat head we just et was sho nuff good child.

Yeah that guy was real tasty, especially the bull's sperm on top of his jughead. Wow, that dish was better I'll bet than those heads we got cheated out of they stole for that traveling lecture room.

Yeah Matthew, the other pig said. You know that guy's got me running.

Well there's a piece of paper over there in the mud, maybe you can wipe with that.

Waldo made it on all fours to the piece of paper lying in the mud.

Hey it's a note that dropped out of the guy's pocket we just made mincemeat of. O an imperial note from the Pope. It looks important.

The two pigs placed their right hoofs to their chests.

Think I could use it? Nobody in this town; it's becoming a ghost town. Besides ain't no Pope suppose to be visiting the States until New York 1966 . . .

The startled pigs looked at each other.

Hey, this creepy town, let's get out of here.

The two pigs with tails curled hoofed it towards the Black Forest surrounding Yellow Back Radio and the sun began to set as it rained on the note in the swinepit behind the gallows:

> It has lately come to our ears, afflicting us with bitter sorrow, that many persons have abandoned themselves to devils, and by their incantations spells and other charms and crafts have slain human infants as well as the offspring of cattle, have withered the crops of the earth the grapes of the vine the fruit of the trees. Men women beasts of burden herd beasts and animals with terrible aches and sore disease. They outrage the Divine Majesty and are the cause of scandal and danger to very many.

> Arriving tomorrow with tool box.

● ○

Loop Garoo, whiplashing the green horse, galloped furiously to a cliff overlooking the sea. He could see the Pope's ship heading towards the horizon, oars rowing in steady rhythm and the shields of his guard reflecting the dim rays of the setting sun.

Loop hesitated on his horse for a moment then, still in the saddle, plunged in. With his rider fastened to him the animal swam towards the Pope's ship which was heading back to its point of origin.

Man and horse overboard! came a cry from the crow's nest.

The Pope chomping on a havana rushed to the ship's railing. Well I'll be damned, and hallelujah, here comes the Loop, the Pontiff smiled. Thomas Jefferson was out of a job but that was O.K. too.

Oakland, California, June 1968

DALKEY ARCHIVE PAPERBACKS

PIERRE ALBERT-BIROT, *Grabinoulor.*

YUZ ALESHKOVSKY, *Kangaroo.*

FELIPE ALFAU, *Chromos.*

Locos.

Sentimental Songs.

ALAN ANSEN,

Contact Highs: Selected Poems 1957-1987.

DJUNA BARNES, *Ladies Almanack.*

Ryder.

JOHN BARTH, *LETTERS.*

Sabbatical.

AUGUSTO ROA BASTOS, *I the Supreme.*

ANDREI BITOV, *Pushkin House.*

ROGER BOYLAN, *Killoyle.*

CHRISTINE BROOKE-ROSE, *Amalgamemnon.*

GERALD BURNS, *Shorter Poems.*

GABRIELLE BURTON, *Heartbreak Hotel.*

MICHEL BUTOR,

Portrait of the Artist as a Young Ape.

JULIETA CAMPOS,

The Fear of Losing Eurydice.

ANNE CARSON, *Eros the Bittersweet.*

LOUIS-FERDINAND CÉLINE, *Castle to Castle.*

London Bridge.

North.

Rigadoon.

HUGO CHARTERIS, *The Tide Is Right.*

JEROME CHARYN, *The Tar Baby.*

MARC CHOLODENKO, *Mordechai Schamz.*

EMILY HOLMES COLEMAN,

The Shutter of Snow.

ROBERT COOVER, *A Night at the Movies.*

STANLEY CRAWFORD,

Some Instructions to My Wife.

RENÉ CREVEL, *Putting My Foot in It.*

RALPH CUSACK, *Cadenza.*

SUSAN DAITCH, *Storytown.*

PETER DIMOCK,

A Short Rhetoric for Leaving the Family.

COLEMAN DOWELL, *Island People.*

Too Much Flesh and Jabez.

RIKKI DUCORNET, *The Complete Butcher's Tales.*

The Fountains of Neptune.

The Jade Cabinet.

Phosphor in Dreamland.

The Stain.

WILLIAM EASTLAKE, *Castle Keep.*

Lyric of the Circle Heart.

STANLEY ELKIN, *Boswell: A Modern Comedy.*

Criers and Kibitzers, Kibitzers and Criers.

The Dick Gibson Show.

The MacGuffin.

ANNIE ERNAUX, *Cleaned Out.*

LAUREN FAIRBANKS, *Muzzle Thyself.*

Sister Carrie.

LESLIE A. FIEDLER,

Love and Death in the American Novel.

RONALD FIRBANK, *Complete Short Stories.*

FORD MADOX FORD, *The March of Literature.*

JANICE GALLOWAY, *Foreign Parts.*

The Trick Is to Keep Breathing.

WILLIAM H. GASS, *The Tunnel.*

Willie Masters' Lonesome Wife.

ETIENNE GILSON, *The Arts of the Beautiful.*

C. S. GISCOMBE, *Giscome Road.*

Here.

KAREN ELIZABETH GORDON, *The Red Shoes.*

PATRICK GRAINVILLE, *The Cave of Heaven.*

GEOFFREY GREEN, ET AL, *The Vineland Papers.*

JIŘÍ GRUŠA, *The Questionnaire.*

JOHN HAWKES, *Whistlejacket.*

ALDOUS HUXLEY, *Antic Hay.*

Point Counter Point.

Those Barren Leaves.

Time Must Have a Stop.

GERT JONKE, *Geometric Regional Novel.*

TADEUSZ KONWICKI, *A Minor Apocalypse.*

The Polish Complex.

ELAINE KRAF, *The Princess of 72nd Street.*

EWA KURYLUK, *Century 21.*

DEBORAH LEVY, *Billy and Girl.*

JOSÉ LEZAMA LIMA, *Paradiso.*

OSMAN LINS, *The Queen of the Prisons of Greece.*

ALF MAC LOCHLAINN,

The Corpus in the Library.

Out of Focus.

D. KEITH MANO, *Take Five.*

BEN MARCUS, *The Age of Wire and String.*

WALLACE MARKFIELD, *Teitlebaum's Window.*

DAVID MARKSON, *Collected Poems.*

Reader's Block.

Springer's Progress.

Wittgenstein's Mistress.

CARL R. MARTIN, *Genii Over Salzburg.*

CAROLE MASO, *AVA.*

HARRY MATHEWS, *Cigarettes.*

The Conversions.

The Journalist.

Visit our website: www.dalkeyarchive.com

DALKEY ARCHIVE PAPERBACKS

Visit our website: www.dalkeyarchive.com

Dalkey Archive Press
ISU Campus Box 4241, Normal, IL 61790–4241
fax (309) 438–7422